Paul is looking for the perfect woman to give his family's ancestral ring.

"Oh, how lovely. . ." Kristen said dreamily.

"The ring has come to symbolize their love and faith."

"But," she swiveled her head to look up at him, "I still don't understand why my aunt gave you a woman's ring?"

"There is more about the ring. It is to be worn only by married or engaged women of the Vasilias family and since I was a member of the family by being your Aunt Aphrodite's godson, and since she had no idea where you were, she gave it to me to put on the finger of my bride."

Kristen sat up straight. To fall in love in one afternoon was one thing but to talk about marriage all in the same afternoon was something entirely different, especially after the disaster of her marriage to Ted.

"Paul. . ." she began, but he cut her off with a chuckle that instantly relieved her.

"Don't worry, Kristen. . .I'm not proposing. . ."

She glanced over at him and at his warm smile, smiled self-conciously back at him. "It's just that. . .we have so much ahead of us. . .my aunt. . .our search. . ."

"I agree."

"You do? Honestly?"

"I do. Even though I know that I'm no longer falling in love with you. . ."

MELANIE PANAGIOTOPOULOS is a native of Virginia who now makes her home in Athens, Greece, with her husband and two children. *Odyssey of Love* is her first inspirational romance novel.

Odyssey
of Love

Melanie Panagiotopoulos

Heartsong Presents

To my dear husband George,
with whom I travel...
"the path of life..."
With love, Melanie

A note from the Author:
I love to hear from my readers! You may write to me at
the following address: **Melanie Panagiotopoulos**
Author Relations
P.O. Box 719
Uhrichsville, OH 44683

All scripture quotations, unless otherwise indicated, are taken from the HOLY BIBLE, NEW INTERNATIONAL VERSION®. NIV®. Copyright © 1973, 1978, 1984 by International Bible Society. Used by permission of Zondervan Publishing House. All rights reserved.

ISBN 1-57748-048-1

ODYSSEY OF LOVE

Cover illustration by Chris Cocozza.

PRINTED IN THE U.S.A.

one

The *tap, tap, tap* of Kristen King's high-heeled shoes irrationally irritated her as she crossed the marble lobby of the downtown San Francisco hotel where she worked as marketing director. The sharp repetition echoed loudly in the hushed elegance of the building and seemed an intrusion, an invasion of the refined surroundings, and even worse, it called attention to Kristen, something she avoided.

Kristen slowed her walk as she approached the reception desk and the tapping receded, relieving her.

But attention had already been drawn to her by the information receptionist who pointed her out to the tall man inquiring as to the location of her office.

Standing away from the information desk, hands in the pockets of his three-piece, ash-gray business suit, the man named Paul Andrakos watched Kristen King with dark, assessing eyes.

Paul had not been sure what to expect when he had decided to travel the 11,000 miles around the world in order to find his godmother's long-lost niece. But the refined, cool beauty of the tall woman leaning across the reception desk surprised him.

His male eyes lingered over the shiny texture of her sable hair, pulled back into some type of skillful knot away from her face. Then they traveled down the long, shapely length of her body to the tip of her black leather pumps, and for the first time since his godmother, Aphrodite, had mentioned her wish to meet her niece, Paul felt the older woman had made the right decision. Kristen King was a woman Paul Andrakos wanted to meet as well.

Kristen turned away from the reception desk and walked in the direction of the imposing doors of the hotel. Paul fell into step behind her. She had the bearing of a queen and yet something about the nape of her neck seemed vulnerable to him. It was velvety and soft, and he found himself wanting to slide his face close to it, smell it, taste it, feel it. He wanted to remove the pins that kept her long hair tight against her head and to cover her neck, protect it, protect her.

Paul breathed out deeply.

He had known more than his fair share of the world's beautiful, and so-called sophisticated women, and knowledge of them had made him cynical. The health of his bank balance and the mystique behind his profession attracted women like flowers do bees. And although most didn't know it, and even fewer would suspect it, Paul was stung to know that these qualities were his strongest draw to the opposite sex. What Paul believed and how he felt about things were both of minor importance to the women he had known. This experience had jaded him.

It had been a while since Paul had seen a woman across a room and felt that special urge to want to know her in that deep, giving way that made for a special relationship. It had been even longer since he had done anything about that urge, not wanting to chance being disappointed yet again. But watching Kristen as she strode, tall and elegant, purposefully in front of him, that desire was definitely there and it was signaling strongly for her. Paul especially liked the idea that Kristen King didn't know a thing about him, his work, or his monetary assets. For once, Paul felt at an advantage. He knew more about an attractive woman than she did about him.

But before he could think about her in those terms he had to ascertain if she was a woman to be trusted with knowledge about her Aunt Aphrodite, his godmother.

Paul's long stride brought him up next to Kristen.

"Excuse me? Ms. King?" he asked.

Kristen cringed inwardly as she heard her name called. Her thoughts had already walked out the hotel doors, if not her body, so to turn and confront an unknown and very attractive man, a man who already was doing something to her equilibrium, was more than she wanted to tackle at the moment. But business was business, she was still in the hotel, and even though she would have like to have avoided this gentleman, she had no choice but to respond to him.

"Yes? May I help you?" A frown cut across her pale forehead as she considered that he looked vaguely familiar, but just as quickly Kristen was sure that she had never before met him. With thick hair, the color of old gold, and eyes that were like finely polished chestnuts, he wasn't a man whom a woman was ever likely to forget—not even Kristen, who had been hurt badly by the man who widowed her, and who had subsequently avoided all involvement with men like one avoids a head-on collision.

"I'm Paul Andrakos," he extended his hand, and a collision was exactly what Kristen felt inside herself when she looked up his considerable height into the darkness of his eyes.

Kristen took Paul's hand. The embrace felt good, he had a firm handshake, a handshake to be trusted. But Kristen had not trusted anybody in a very long time.

"Andrakos? . . . A Greek name?" she questioned, quick to cover with small talk the attraction she felt for him. It was a skill she had perfected during the last few years of her twenty-eight years of life.

"Definitely," Paul affirmed and smiled, a friendly smile, and yet Kristen thought that it was a careful smile as well. Their hands parted but not their eyes. His continued to hold hers. They narrowed and made Kristen feel as if he were measuring her up, but not in a sexual way, and not in a business way either. This assessment did not offend Kristen, only puzzle her.

"I need to talk to you," he paused, "about family business."

"Family business. . ." she echoed quickly, caught off guard. That was the last thing she expected to hear and her eyes widened as her mind started to run wildly through that all too familiar nightmarish maze which she thought she had left far behind her when she had left Virginia for good.

"You're from Virginia?" she asked, her deep voice little

more than a whisper.

"No, from Greece," Paul replied, and only then did Kristen realize that his accent was not American. It was a lot like her father's had been, a mixture of Greek and English.

"My father was from Greece." She automatically made small talk, giving herself time to think. Her left hand moved to the gold chain hanging around her neck and she kneaded it between her fingers, something she did when agitated, frightened or confused. But there were very few people left in the world who knew that, and definitely not the man standing in front of her.

"Yes, I know," he replied flatly, his accent softening the definitive knowledge of his words.

Startled, Kristen tilted her head, and Paul watched the changing expressions that crossed her face. First confusion, then fear, covered her clear, green eyes, but uniting them was strength. They combined to give her the appearance of a beautiful doe that wanted to run but was too curious and too smart to do so. And, as Paul watched her, he saw the exact moment when understanding replaced all other emotions.

"You're from my aunt," she pronounced. Kristen spoke the words slowly, knowing that there could be no other explanation, and Paul liked how it was a statement about something obvious and not an empty, airy question.

The corners of his mouth deepened. "Yes. Your Aunt Aphrodite. Your father's older sister," he affirmed, and motioned over toward a secluded section of the lobby where comfortable sofas were discreetly placed among plants. He asked, "May we talk?"

Kristen nodded her head thoughtfully, and squeezing her shoulder bag close to her side said, "I think we'd better."

Turning, she led the way to the furthest, most private corner of the lobby.

The only connection Kristen had with Greece was this aunt whose existence she had only discovered while going through her parents' papers after their sudden deaths three months earlier. Kristen had called her, feeling that, regardless of the reason behind the siblings' decades-long estrangement, her aunt would want to know, indeed had a right to know, about her brother's death. Kristen hadn't talked to her aunt but to a man who had said that her aunt would get in touch with her. But as the long months passed and Kristen received no word, she'd assumed that her aunt didn't want anything to do with her and that the estrangement was to continue into her generation.

That realization had hurt.

Not having any other relatives in the world put an emphasis on blood relatives which most people ignored and made this surprise aunt of great importance to Kristen. Knowing that there was someone else in the world to whom she was related had given Kristen a warm feeling, a feeling that had died, however, with the passing of the days, days which had brought no word from her aunt.

Arriving at the plush, forest green sofas, Kristen sat in the corner of one, crossing her legs in front of her. She watched as Paul Andrakos folded himself into the close corner of an adjacent one. Again, that vague, nickering feeling that she knew him from somewhere crossed her mind. But she pushed the thought aside. It was unimportant; his reason for coming was all that mattered.

Life had taught Kristen to be direct, so she asked, "Mr. Andrakos, it's been nearly three months since I called my aunt. Why has it taken her so long to contact me?"

Paul liked her straightforward way of speaking so he replied equally directly, not bothering to mince his words. "She's been a very sick lady, Ms. King."

"Sick?" Kristen echoed dismay, as the fingers of her left hand again found the chain around her neck. In her insecurity, the thought had never occurred to her that her aunt might have been ill.

Paul nodded. "That's why I'm here, and not your aunt. Believe me, if she could travel she would be sitting here with you today, not me."

Kristen shook her head. After convincing herself that she was unwanted and totally unblessed where family relationships were concerned, it amazed her to consider that there just might be a relative, someone who had the same blood flowing in her veins, with whom she could have a relationship. "I'm sorry. . .I had no idea. . .the man I talked to didn't tell me that she was ill."

The corners of Paul's mouth deepened. He loved his god-mother with a love normally only reserved for mothers, but he was surprised to discover that Kristen King's response to his next words was important to him for more reasons than just those pertaining to his godmother; it was important to him on a personal level as well.

"Ms. King, she wasn't sick until hearing that your parents had died." He paused. "It was that shock which caused her to suffer a heart attack."

Kristen's eyes shut for several moments and when she opened them, the pain that Paul read in their watery green depths was real, and it impressed him. It impressed him that she should feel so strongly for a woman whom she had never met; it impressed him more than a million words spoken on her behalf ever could have, and with it that old cynicism that was as hard as a block of marble and had been a part of him for so long that he had thought it was a permanent trait of his personality, started being chipped away at the edges. He liked the light way that it made him feel.

"I'm sorry. . .I had no idea," she finally whispered.

"None of us did." He stated simply. "If we had known that it would affect her so deeply, to the detriment of her health, we wouldn't have told her. At least, we would have found another way to do so," he offered. Kristen's reaction was far more caring and concerned than he had thought possible. But Paul was comparing her to the women he knew. And he was beginning to realize that there was no comparison. There was a lot more to Kristen King than business brawn and physical beauty and this thought pleased him.

"When I didn't hear from my aunt," Kristen hesitantly spoke in a voice lightly flavored with a soft, southern accent, "I thought that she didn't want to have anything to do with me.

I'd resigned myself to the thought." Her shoulders shrugged minutely beneath her purple silk blouse and they seemed very fragile to Paul, as if they had carried too much weight for far too long.

And too, the vulnerability of her words amazed him. Vulnerability and humility. It was in her giving green eyes, in the softness of her deep voice, in the air around her, and with an insight born from years of reading people Paul was now quite certain that Kristen King would never do anything to hurt his godmother. Ironically, he found himself hoping that his godmother, a formidable personality even when ill, would never hurt Kristen.

As if he'd been doing it forever, he reached across the arm of the sofa and took her long slender hand in his own, gently squeezing it.

Kristen surprised herself by accepting his hand, accepting it as she might a gift. It was a natural reflex, born of an emotional moment and she pressed her fingers against the palm of his hand.

She liked the feeling. She needed it.

"Ms. King," he leaned forward, "your aunt was pleased that you called her, but extremely saddened by your news. I don't know what it was that kept your father and aunt apart all those years, but did you know that they had resolved their differences and that your parents were planning a trip to Greece?"

She smiled, a small little smile that tugged at his awakening feelings for her. "I'm glad, glad for them all."

He nodded and expelling a deep breath, glanced at his watch. "I'd like to take you to lunch. There is much that we have to discuss. Can you get away?" He hadn't planned on asking her out, but neither had he planned on her affecting him the way she did.

Kristen nodded her head. "Yes, I. . ." but then she stopped, and shook her head. Giving his hand a quick squeeze, a sort of thank you, she let go of it and lightly touched her fingers to her hair. "I forgot. . .I have a hairdresser's appointment."

"A hairdresser's appointment?" he echoed. It seemed so mundane and out of place after the import of their discussion. "Why?"

"To cut my hair." She answered simply and thought how it was absurd for her to be discussing her hair with a man who was practically a stranger. Absurd. . .but kind of fun as well.

His eyebrows lifted and he gazed at her deeply and reflectively in a way in which a very close friend might.

It was as he looked at her so poetically that Kristen realized why he looked familiar to her. . .and she had to stifle a laugh as it dawned on her. The coincidence of it all was outrageous!

For Paul Andrakos didn't resemble anyone she knew, rather, he resembled a thing. . .a work of art. . .a statue actually. . .He looked like her replica of the *Youth of Antikythera* which sat on her living-room coffee table in her home across the bay.

The actual, life-size statue of bronze had been found in an ancient shipwreck off the coast of the little island of Antikythera in the Gulf of Crete, just northwest of the island of Crete, and was now displayed in the National Archaeological Museum of Greece in Athens. Kristen's good friend, Lottie, an archaeologist now living in Greece, had visited Kristen the previous summer and brought her an official replica of the museum piece.

Lottie faced life lightly in a fun, carefree way. Indicative of her personality, when she gave Kristen the statue she had declared, "Now all you need to do is find a real live fellow like this statue. . .or maybe one who has aged during the last twenty-four hundred years and is now a *man*, and not a youth of nineteen." She had laughed loudly, proud of her joke, and pointedly ignored the fact that they both knew that Kristen had absolutely no desire to get involved with a man.

But Kristen had accepted the gift in the spirit in which it had been given. Her friend had been trying to help her in the only way she knew how, in the humorous, light sort of way in which she herself faced life's problems, and Kristen had loved her for it.

Kristen remembered squeezing the foot-high statue to her chest and replying, "No, I think I'll just become friends with this little fellow. I already know that his heart is made of bronze so he can never hurt mine."

The funny thing was, in the months that followed, her little statue of the *Youth of Antikythera* had become like a silent pet to Kristen, a friend whom she talked to at the end of the day, kind of like most people talk to cats and dogs.

Looking at the man before her, Kristen decided that he could have been an older version of the model for the statue. His thick wavy hair and long straight nose and the sensitive set of his facial bone structure were identical with the statue's, but even more, the look he now sent to her was an eternal one, one which, like the *Youth of Antikythera,* tried hard to read the workings of another's soul. He wasn't trying to figure out how she would look with her hair down, but rather, why she would want to cut it.

"Don't cut it," he finally said decisively and Kristen couldn't stifle her laugh any longer.

She laughed, a light, carefree, bubbly laugh, and Paul laughed with her, and as they laughed Kristen realized that she hadn't enjoyed herself so much in a very long time. Before the fiasco of her marriage she had enjoyed a good time, good spur-of-the-moment fun, just as she was enjoying it now, immensely.

"Don't cut your hair," he repeated, his eyes still twinkling with laughter and his smile, a beautiful, dazzling smile, different from the one he had previously given, seemed to make the whole world right.

Grinning back at him, her mouth somehow unable to do anything else, Kristen wanted to ask "Why?" What possible difference could it make to him whether she cut her hair or not? But discussing her hair with a man who was still practically a stranger couldn't be any stranger than comparing him to her pet statue, and yet somehow it all seemed nice too. On the tail of such deep thoughts and questions about her parents and long-lost Aunt Aphrodite, frivolous thoughts were very nice and something Kristen hadn't had in a long, long time.

She rolled her eyes self-consciously, her lips still turned up in a smile. "Well, I won't cut it today anyway. Let me call and cancel my appointment and then I'll be right with you." She stood and his considerable height politely followed suit.

Reaching out, his fingers lightly touched her upper arm, detaining her. Through the silkiness of her blouse, his fingers felt warm to Kristen, and nice. . .really nice.

"Thank you, Ms. King. Thank you for changing your plans." His voice was both husky and elegant, like a caress. And although the laughter was gone from his voice, something just as important, something even more important was now there. Now there was friendship, a new and budding friendship in his words.

Kristen shook her head. "No, I must thank you for coming." She licked her lips and continued hesitantly, wondering how much she should tell him of her feelings. But looking at him she felt that she could say what she really felt. So she did.

"I. . .was really sad when I thought that I had been ignored by my aunt. I don't have any other living relatives and, well . . .it's important to me to learn about my father's sister."

He nodded and she knew that she hadn't made a mistake in trusting him. "Your aunt feels exactly the same way about you, Ms. King."

"I'm so glad. . .but please, call me Kristen."

"Kristen," he repeated, as if he were tasting it, and the soft inflections of his accent made her name sound musical, magical to her. "A lovely name. And I'm Paul."

"Paul," she said and their eyes seemed to fuse together; deep brown ones merged with crystal green ones and with their merging Kristen's heart pounded against her rib cage. It wanted freedom from the prison in which she had placed it when her husband died a year and a half ago on their wedding day. A little freedom in that age-old game of male and female was all that it wanted, and Kristen decided as she stood there that for this one afternoon she would give it that freedom.

Paul Andrakos was safe after all. He lived in far-off Greece.

After today she probably wouldn't ever see him again. It was time for her to start trusting again; time to start, by trusting her own heart.

"I'll only be a moment," she said, and smiling, swiveled away from him to cross over to the reception desk.

This time the tap, tap, tap of her heels against the marble floor didn't bother her. And neither did she mind the idea of Paul Andrakos's eyes following her as she walked with the feminine tap across the lobby. She could feel his dark eyes on her back and a very womanly part of her, a part that had lain dormant for a very long time, hoped that he liked what he saw.

She reached for the phone at the reception desk and turned to watch the tall length of Paul Andrakos as he made a phone call from the telephone on the table next to the sofa. *Such thick golden hair and dark, dark eyes, eyes a person could trust, eyes a person's soul could fall into,* she thought. He was a golden Greek, just like her father had been before his head had turned white. But there the resemblance ended. The budding feelings she had for Paul Andrakos were definitely not like those she had had for her father.

She was attracted to Paul Andrakos in that age-old, inexplicable way that a woman is attracted to a particular man. She admitted it to herself, for she also reasoned that he was a safe attraction. He would soon return to his end of the world, and the only remembrances she would have of him would be of letting herself open up to the world once again and that of her little statue of the *Youth of Antikythera* on her coffee table in her home above the Pacific ocean, who would from now on remind her of the real live 'Man from Greece' who had come with information about her aunt.

Yes, she thought, just before her secretary came on the line and she directed her to cancel her hairdresser's appointment, *Paul Andrakos was a safe attraction. . .for one afternoon.*

Hanging up the phone, she watched as he casually strode toward her. Squaring her shoulders, she took a deep breath like one normally does before plunging into a cold pool, and clutching her shoulder bag to her side walked forward to meet him.

"All set?" he asked.

She nodded her head and breathed out. "Did you want to dine here in the hotel? There's an excellent roof garden restaurant."

I just made reservations at a little restaurant I know of on the wharf. Is that all right with you?"

"What, with the competition?" she teased, and smiling, he took her hand and, as if he had been doing it forever, tucked it among the folds of his expensive suit into the crook of his elbow and guided her toward the massive doors of the hotel.

It surprised Kristen that he had taken her arm but she didn't feel offended. She knew from her father that it was a European habit. Her father used to always walk this way with her and her mother. Besides, it felt so good to have someone else directing her steps for a change. She'd been fending for herself for so long that even this one moment of following someone else was a treat, and the fact that her hand felt so perfect upon his arm, so natural and right, made it even more of one.

As they crossed the lobby, she took the moment to observe that he was tall and broad, but not like an American football player who is normally massive. Rather, Paul Andrakos was slender like a swimmer with a body that was shaped to knife swiftly through the water with the grace and ease of the clipper ships of old. She mused that the water, or something to do with the water, must be the natural setting for this man. It seemed to be a part of him.

So absorbed was Kristen in her thoughts that she failed to greet the two gentlemenly doormen as she breezed through on Paul's arm. Her transformation, however, did not go unnoticed by their ever-seeing, ever-observant eyes. They were accustomed to seeing the beautiful young executive with the sculptured expression nod an acknowledgement to them as she entered or exited the hotel. They gave one another knowing looks as she floated by with her escort and weren't offended that she failed to salute them. Her face was that of a woman now, one definitely not made of stone. It pleased the elderly gentlemen, who had always felt a bit sad for her.

two

The warm summertime wind buffeted Kristen and Paul, and the traffic of the city roared around them as they stepped out of the protection of the marquee. It thrilled Kristen. She had loved San Francisco from the very first day that she'd arrived a little over a year ago. The city never failed to bring her senses alive with its vibrancy and color and Paul Andrakos seemed to combine forces with the city to doubly assault her.

Leaning close to her he spoke into her ear, and she felt her nerves quiver like a tuning fork just struck.

"Shall I hail a cab? Or would you like to walk and catch a cable car down to the wharf?"

Eyes shining, pleased that he would think to ask, she readily answered him, "Oh. . .I love cable cars!"

"I somehow thought you would," Paul smiled and started guiding her down the street.

She smiled up at him, and as the wind whipped the clean spicy fragrance of his aftershave around her, she found herself enjoying the manly fragrance that was him, masculine and fresh and nice.

Turning a corner, a gust of Pacific wind whipped through the tall buildings of the street like it might through a deep, deep canyon in the wilds, and Kristen's prim pleated skirt billowed out, soaring high above her knees. Startled, she frantically grabbed out for the wayward fabric.

Trying to be helpful Paul reached over to assist her, but when his hand inadvertently brushed against her leg, his help became much more than that, and with it Kristen's heart flew every bit as out of control as the silky folds of her skirt had.

Careful not to touch his hand, she relieved his long fingers of the material which he had captured. Their eyes, however, touched and held, became captive as they stood in the middle

18

of the sidewalk looking deeply at one another.

Like in a melodramatic video clip, the multitude of people around them—those on the sidewalk walking, those in cars driving, and even those in a helicopter flying high in the sky above them—disappeared and only the music that came from their souls remained.

They were the only ones on that street, their attraction for one another was the only sound heard where man and woman recognized that there was something special between their particular souls, something very, very special.

With a silence that spoke loudly, the man called Paul and the woman called Kristen vaguely recognized that they needed one another to travel the path of life. The proverbial "love at first sight"—or at least almost first sight—had hit them.

But where this thought was appealing to Paul, it scared Kristen and she again reminded Paul of a beautiful doe unsure of the path to follow.

Wanting to relieve the fear he read in her eyes, he smiled, and reaching for her hand again tucked it in the crook of his arm and guided her down the sidewalk acting as though nothing had passed between them, as though nothing had happened.

"What a wind!" he expostulated.

"I. . .I normally wear tighter skirts or even slacks on days when the wind is blowing," she said, wanting to forget the moment, to forget the unspoken revelation which had passed between them.

He chuckled and pointed down to her skirt which was still trying to fly free of her hand, "I can understand why."

Relieved, she couldn't help the small laugh which escaped her lips. "But I like the wind. It's exhilarating."

"Then you would like Athens when the Meltemia starts to blow."

"Meltemia?" She tilted her head questioningly, glad for any conversation that might help calm her. The attraction that she felt for this man and which she was now certain he felt for her was a little bit more than she wanted to tackle at this point in her life. If she didn't know that he lived on the other side of the earth, and that she probably wouldn't see him again after today. . .well, she wasn't sure what she would do.

"Meltemia are winds that blow down from the cool zones of Russia to fill a vacuum created by the hot air rising over the Sahara desert to the south of Greece," he answered. "They are a lot like your Californian Santa Ana winds. They start blowing with the rising of the sun and end with its setting, acting as nature's fan to cool the earth and cleanse it."

"Winds from Russia. . .the Sahara Desert. . ." she murmured. "Sounds so exotic somehow."

"Not any more so than your Santa Ana winds sound to me. In Europe, California, especially San Francisco, is thought of as paradise on earth."

Looking out over the Golden Gate, the entrance mouth to San Francisco Bay, with the tall Golden Gate Bridge spanning it, and to the sailboats with their colorful spinnakers dotting the deep blue sea beneath it, Kristen couldn't help but understand people comparing it to paradise. It was one of the world's most beautiful locations and yet, even though her moving to its welcoming shores had helped to put her life back on track after the horrible events of her marriage, she knew that it wasn't paradise, and shaking her head thoughtfully she spoke softly, almost wistfully. "No. . .not even this is paradise. . .I don't think paradise is to be found anywhere on earth."

With matching seriousness Paul responded, "I quite agree."

Startled, and yet pleased, she turned to him. "You do?"

As they paused on a busy corner waiting for the walk signal to appear, he nodded and his mouth quirked slightly, in a way that seemed pessimistic to Kristen. "I've seen enough of life to know that what people run after all their lives—monetary success, social standing, good looks, holidays—doesn't bring the happiness people assume it should. But I believe that—" he broke off and flashed her a guilty smile. "I'm sorry, I didn't mean to bore you," he waved his response away into the wind as they started to cross the street.

"No. . .please go on," she encouraged him as they weaved around people in the crosswalk, and Paul was amazed to think that he had finally found a woman who was interested in what he believed, not just what he did for a living. A frown cut across his face as he vaguely wondered if she cared because she didn't know anything else about him, and he wondered if she would continue to care if she did know his financial status. The thought of never having monetary worries was very appealing to the women he had met. But then, remembering what he had learned about Kristen, he knew that money had never been a problem for her either.

Kristen misread his frown and thought he was embarrassed to speak his mind, so she again prompted him. "Please. . .I'd like to know what you believe."

"Why?" he looked down at her, his brow a quizzical line slicing across his forehead. "You hardly know me."

She knew that what he said was true, but she also knew that he would soon be leaving and that made such a deep discussion easier than it would be with a person who lived close by to her. She licked her lips and replied truthfully, "Sometimes, it's easier to talk to someone you don't know very well about really important things than people you do know. . .there are no preconceived notions to deal with, no histories to take into account. . . ."

He nodded his agreement.

"So please tell me what you were going to say," she prompted with a smile that made Paul feel more carefree than he had felt in a long time and happy to speak of his deep, deep yearnings.

"Well, I think that there has to be Something More, Something More in life which brings us a little bit closer to that Paradise which we all seek."

"I agree. . ." she frowned thoughtfully while tucking a wayward strand of hair behind her ear. "But what is that elusive 'Something More'?"

"I don't know. . .something to do with our souls, I think." He looked down at her and smiled sheepishly. "Sounds funny,

I know. But it's something I'm determined to someday seek and find."

"That's something I'd like to find as well," she replied softly, truthfully.

He smiled and squeezed her hand as they arrived at the cable car stop and waited for the car to come. He didn't release her hand and Kristen didn't ask for it back. "You know, Kristen, I think you're the first woman I've ever met who feels as I do."

"Most likely other women have felt this need but they have superficially coated and hidden it with the things you mentioned before—monetary success, social standing, etc. . . ."

"Have you ever done that?"

Have I? Kristen wondered as she let her eyes drift out beyond his shoulder over the busy street. Thoughtfully, she shook her head and turned her gaze back to his. "Not really, but I think this need was fulfilled for me by my parents. We were very close. After they. . .were killed in the boating accident. . .well. . .I've come to realize that there has to be, as you said, Something More in life. Something that doesn't depend on people. . .or things. . .or work. . . ." She shook her head and turned to look out toward the bay. "Something. . ." she finished wistfully.

"Do you think that Something might be God?" he asked softly and she turned her eyes back to him.

"It might be. I just wish I knew how to find out."

Frowning, he replied, "I would say church but I don't know. I've been kind of discouraged by some people I know who go to church every Sunday and every religious holiday but then hurt their fellow human beings the rest of the time."

She remembered that her "almost" husband's family had been religious churchgoers and they had been the primary instigators in hurting her after Ted's car had run off the cliff the night of their wedding. They were the reason she'd left Virginia and missed spending the last year of her parents' lives with them.

She grimaced. "Yeah. . .me too."

He chuckled and squeezed her hand between both of his.

"We're kind of a case of the blind, leading the blind, I'd say."

She smiled in agreement and placed her other hand over his. "Well, we might be blind, but at least we know that we have to go somewhere—that there is something unknown which we must find."

"Maybe. . .we can grope our way. . .together," he said softly, his accent making the unromantic words seem more romantic than any she had ever heard before and because of this, more frightening as well.

As if his hands suddenly burned hers she let go of them and laughed, a fake sound even to her own ears, "How? By e-mail? You live on the other side of the world remember?" And as the moment was getting to be too much for her, she was once again glad that he did. But his next words shattered her false sense of safety.

"Kristen. . ." he spoke hesitantly, softly, and with hope in his dark eyes, "your Aunt Aphrodite was hoping. . .that you would travel to Greece to visit her. . ."

"What?!"

He quickly continued. "This is why I've come. To ask you to visit her and to accompany you to Greece."

The clang, clang, clang of the cable car as it careened around the corner toward their stop wasn't any louder than the ringing in Kristen's temples. It wasn't that she didn't want to meet her aunt. She did. She just wasn't sure that she wanted to go any further with Paul Andrakos than to lunch at Fisherman's Wharf.

The safe world she had built for herself on the shores of the Pacific Ocean seemed to be rocking and swaying as if in a strong earthquake and, like one experiencing an earthquake, she wasn't sure which direction to go, if any, in order to escape it.

The cable car came to a stop in front of them. Rotely, she stepped onto the running board and, as she did so, she looked with longing back at the road she had just walked. She some-how knew that there was no going back. Her path had been mapped out for her and, unknowing as to how it was to change her life, she had walked it. As happy as the last few moments had been, she wished that she hadn't agreed to lunch with Paul Andrakos. She was terrified of the unknown and of being disappointed by people yet again.

"Kristen," Paul's voice came to her through the rattling of the car as it started to move away on its track. "You don't have to decide now."

She looked at him sheepishly, the wind from the moving car carrying her soft but truthful words back to him, "It's just that everything is happening so suddenly after months of nothing."

Without her intending it there was double meaning in her words and he realized it.

"I know."

She nodded and stepped inside to sit on a protected bench. He sat down next to her, draping his arm casually without touching her across the back of the bench. Wanting time to get her thoughts in order, Kristen decided to play tour guide. "Did you know that the first cable cars were built in 1873, and that they are still painted with the exact same colors as they were then?"

"More than a hundred years. . .that's quite a long time when you think that San Francisco isn't a very old city."

She laughed. "I guess by Greek standards it's a very young city."

"Young and beautiful," he agreed, and the look he gave her left no doubt that he was referring to more than just the city.

She quickly continued to find refuge in her role of tour guide. "Yes, well. . .there is a museum with an underground viewing room where people can observe the huge sheaves that guide the cable cars from under the street, too."

"They're amazing contraptions," he agreed, obviously amused by her travel log.

She smiled but boldly continued, "Well. . .Rudyard Kipling liked them. He wrote, 'They take no count of rise or fall, but slide equable on their appointed courses. . .turn corners. . . cross other lines, and for aught I know, may run up the sides of houses.' "

The car chose that moment to turn a corner sharply and Kristen was thrown against Paul. His hand grasped her shoulder to steady her, but when he didn't let go of her after the pace of the cable car evened out, she looked up at him questioningly.

"And how about you, Kristen? Do you slide equably on your appointed course?" His tone was serious, serious and caring.

"I. . ." she looked down at her hands and then back up at him. She wasn't sure how to answer the question. She decided to be truthful, something she was finding very easy to be with this man. "I don't know. I'm not sure what my 'appointed course' should be—I've always tried to do what I think is right. . .but it hasn't always been correct."

None of us knows what our 'appointed course' is," he pointed out kindly.

"I know but. . .at least some of us have an idea of where we're going and what we're going to do with our lives." She grimaced. "My life has made some strange and really nasty turns."

"Do you think going to Greece is a bad turn for you?"

She shook her head. "No. . .but. . .I'm relatively happy here."

"It's safe. Right?"

She lifted her head defiantly. "That's right. It's safe. It's a known in a world which is so full of unknown."

"But what about that Unknown, that Something More that you want to discover. Do you think you'll find it by just staying put?"

Tilting her head up, she replied, "I might."

He nodded. "Yes. You might." He lightly ran his thumb across her cheek. "But Kristen. . .maybe. . .maybe you are meant to travel to Greece. . .to meet your aunt. . .maybe it's all part of your appointed path. Maybe, by not going, you would miss out on the best path of your life."

She sighed. She felt defeated. "I know. I just wish there was someone whom I could ask."

The brakeman pulled the brake lever, bringing the cable car to a screeching halt at their stop on the wharf. Standing, Paul reached out to help Kristen alight from the car. His lips turned up into an amused sort of smile, and as she stepped down onto the sidewalk, he suggested, "Well. . .you could ask your aunt for advice."

She looked up at him in wonder. She liked the way that sounded.

It was nice to know that there was someone to whom she could turn. Smiling broadly, she replied, "Yes, I guess I could."

three

The wharf was busy with tourists and businesspeople, with children riding bikes and with children being pushed in strollers, with street vendors and street performers, and after a woman carrying a "walk-a-way" shrimp cocktail nearly spilled it all on Paul and a man balancing several huge crabs collided with Kristen, the two gave up talking until settled in their restaurant seats, which commanded a frontline view of the bay.

Kristen was surprised to hear the maitre d' address Paul by name but even more surprised to see several heads of well-known businessmen turn in their direction as they made their way across the plush lavender carpet to their table next to the window. "You seem to be known here," she commented as they sat down, and she motioned to a table where the people turned guiltily away as Paul's glance fell upon them.

"I probably just look like someone they know," he suggested.

She looked at him with curious interest and picking up her linen napkin, she laid it across her lap and asked, "What is it that you do anyway?"

"Oh. . .a little bit of this and a little bit of that," he replied offhandedly.

She frowned. His answer bothered her. It was too vague, too glib, something he hadn't been before. Her eyes skimmed out over the busy wharf to the elegant Golden Gate Bridge and then back to the historic Alcatraz Island in the foreground before they again came to rest on the dark eyes of the man seated across from her.

"Paul. . .there's something I don't understand," she reached for the crystal goblet of water and sipped from it. "Why didn't my aunt just call and invite me? Why did you come in person?"

"I have business here in the city—" he prevaricated, but then, looking at her questioning eyes he knew that if they were ever to have a relationship, something he found himself wanting more and more with each passing moment, he'd have to be honest. He knew that the knowledge he had about her had to be in the open between them. Clearing his throat, he sat back in his chair and admitted, "We had heard things—"

"What things?" Icy fingers of dread started to climb up Kristen's spine and she gripped the stem of the goblet tighter.

"We had read things—"

She waited, she knew what was coming and in spite of the air conditioning in the restaurant, she felt herself break out in a cold sweat. Was her almost-marriage to Ted to taint all her future relationships? She knew that the attraction she and Paul felt for one another was something special, something that went far beyond the physical to touch the deep yearnings of their souls. Now that Kristen wondered if she might lose Paul she recognized how desperately she didn't want to, how much she truly wanted to see him again and try for a future. . . together.

He watched the emotions that played across her face. She reminded him of the little tabby cat he'd rescued from the kicks and taunts of nasty children in the center of Athens the week before. Her green eyes were as wary, terrified, and vulnerable as that kitten's had been. The kitten had allowed him to pick her up and bring her home with him. He wondered if Kristen would allow him to do the same thing.

Somehow he managed to find the only words that could save their new friendship, "Kristen, if it makes a difference, I don't believe a word that was written in that newspaper. I don't believe that you were in any way responsible for the death of your new husband. He was drunk. He was driving. He ran off the cliff. Thank God you weren't with him."

She could tell that he meant it and the relief that she felt melted the icy fingers of dread away like the sun breaking out from the clouds on a cool winter day.

"Thank you, Paul," she whispered and wished that she could leave the subject alone but knew that she couldn't, not yet. "But. . .in order to know about. . .the events of my wedding day. . .you must have had me investigated." The idea was appalling to Kristen.

"Yes," he paused. "You were investigated."

Her eyes flashed her anger. "What exactly is going on here?" she demanded, bringing her hand down hard on the table, rattling the silverware. She was terrified that she had once again been a bad judge of character. "Who are you," she ground out, "and what exactly is your relationship to my aunt? Are you her private eye?" she asked sarcastically.

His lips twisted wryly. He was amused by her question. "Well. . .I guess you could say that I am. . .especially where you're concerned."

His obvious amusement only served to further feed her anger. To think that people, people whom she hadn't even met, were spying into her private affairs bothered her. With her soft, southern accent smothering her anger she asked, "Oh. . .what else have you discovered about me?"

He shrugged his shoulders slightly. If he realized that she was angry, he deliberately ignored it and kept the conversation easygoing. "Nothing much actually, except to know that today is your twenty-eighth birthday." He picked up his goblet of water and flashing a smile filled with budding friendship, toasted her. "Happy Birthday, Kristen."

In spite of herself her lips curved upward and she felt her anger fade away. She didn't think anyone in San Francisco would remember her birthday and until that moment, she didn't realize how much it meant to her that someone did. It felt nice to be wished a happy one. "Thank you," she murmured and looked down at the butter on her bread plate, absently noticing that it was shaped like a conch shell. Feeling happy but a little bit uncomfortable, she picked up her dinner roll and asked, "But you still haven't told me what your relationship is to my aunt?"

As she stabbed the conch shell swirl of butter and started to spread it on her roll, she felt him bring his chair closer to the table. "I'm sorry, I should have told you sooner. . .you see. . . your aunt is much more to me than just a friend and a business associate. . .she's my godmother."

Kristen's green eyes widened in wonder. "Your godmother? She's your nona?" Her brows drew together as she remembered some of what her father had taught her about Greek traditions. "Isn't that what you call a godmother in Greek?"

A smile touched his mouth. "Exactly. She's my nona."

Kristen tilted her head, beginning to understand the situation better. "That's quite a strong tie in Greek society, isn't it?"

"It can be," he agreed, still holding her hand.

"Is it where your nona, my aunt, is concerned?" she pressed.

"Very." His tone left no doubt as to the love he felt for his godmother. "I love nona like a mother. Since my parents died, she has been a mother to me," he paused, and squeezed her hand, this time reassuringly. "That's why I had to assure myself of your character before—"

"—before," she sighed and finished for him understanding everything now, "you invited me to come."

"Yes," he nodded his head, relieved that it was out in the open between them. "Nona was too sick to allow someone to come who might upset her."

"And. . .after you read the accounts in that newspaper. . ." she let the rest of the sentence hang wryly.

"That newspaper did a hatchet job on you!" Anger flashed across his face and Kristen decided then that she didn't ever want to be on the receiving end of his anger. "Why? There must be some sort of behind-the-scenes reason. Was the owner of the paper related to your husband in any way?"

She smiled at his astuteness and let go of his hand. "You do know how things work." And then coming to a decision, a decision of trust, she said, "My father-in-law owned the paper."

"Ah. . ." he sat back in his seat, "that says everything."

"Well not everything maybe. . .but enough for the moment."

He eyed her speculatively. He wanted to ask more but it was enough right now that she didn't seem upset with him for checking her out. "So you do understand why I had to come and see for myself what sort of person you are?"

She grimaced. "Well, I can't say I'm thrilled but—I do understand. I probably would have done the same thing had I read such things about someone. Even though I haven't met my aunt, Paul, I care about her. She's the only relative I have left in the world, unless. . ." she paused as it occurred to her that she could possibly have cousins through her aunt. "Does she have any children?"

"No," Paul tilted his head upward which Kristen knew from her father was the Greek expression for no. "She never married."

"Really. . ." Kristen frowned thoughtfully, more and more intrigued with this woman who was her aunt. "I don't claim to know too much about modern Greek culture, but isn't that a bit strange for a Greek woman of her generation?"

Paul's mouth tightened. "Yes, it is unusual, but then your Aunt Aphrodite does not fit into the norm in any respect."

"Tell me about her," Kristen prompted.

"To understand your aunt, you must first know something about modern Greek history."

She sat back as the waiter brought their order of baked Pacific salmon and placed it before them. "Ummm. . .this looks delicious." She savored the lemony aroma and then looked back at Paul as the waiter departed. "Please tell me."

He nodded but motioned to her to eat. She picked up her fork and flaked off a bit of the tender fish, making a stab at eating while he told her about her aunt.

"It has only been a little over forty years that Greece has been without bloodshed on her soil. During Aphrodite's young adulthood, throughout her twenties, there was war on her doorstep.

"First there was World War II, the occupation, and then when most other European countries were pulling themselves back into being working countries, civil war broke out in Greece."

"Civil war? Like we had with the North against the South?" she asked and waited as he took a few bitefuls of the lemony fish.

He shook his head. "No, much worse. The dividing line was ideological, not geographical. It was a war against Communist takeover. . .and the Greek people. . .much to their credit, managed to keep it out of Greece when much of Europe, was cloaked by it."

"I didn't realize. . ."

"This war lasted an additional four years." He sighed. "It is very hard for me to even imagine what life must have been like during that time, but I do know that it had a profound effect on the way that the populace think and act even today." He paused and took a few bites of food.

"I just can't imagine anything so horrible as war at my home either. . ." she murmured and toyed with her food, much too interested in what Paul had to say to eat much.

"Well, most of the women survived by immersing themselves in their families. They were their men's companions and helpers and their children's teachers and caretakers."

"But my aunt?"

He smiled as he thought about the older woman. "Your aunt cast the traditional role from her life and put all of her energies into her work."

"Her work?" Kristen's eyes opened wide in surprise. "What does she do?"

Amazement lurked in his dark eyes. "You really have no idea?"

She shrugged her shoulders. "No. How could I? I didn't even know of her existence until recently," she reminded him.

"I just thought that your father might have said something, something about his past life," he prompted.

"No. Nothing. He never talked about Greece." She shook her head and waited.

Paul chuckled at her innocence. "Kristen, your aunt is one of the most successful persons in Greece, in Europe for that matter."

"What?" she was flabbergasted and repeated, "what does she do?"

"After the war she plunged into learning all she could about the family shipping business."

"Shipping business!"

He nodded, and speaking very softly, explained, "Kristen, you come from a very old and noble shipping family."

"I had no idea." She looked out the window, her savory lunch totally forgotten, and her eyes watched a ship as it passed under the Golden Gate Bridge with an interest she had never felt before. "My father never told me anything. . ."

"Your father too had been trained in the business by your grandfather and he was to have been in charge. When he left, however, Aphrodite took over, although. . ." his lips twisted, "not quite as easily as all that. Your grandfather thought a woman's place was in the home, definitely not in the shipping business."

Kristen rolled her eyes. "I can imagine. . ."

With admiration in his voice, Paul said, "But your aunt is a fighter. . ."

"But. . .what happened between my father and my aunt? Did it have to do with the business?"

"No. The only thing I'm sure of is that it didn't have to do with the business."

"Then why were they estranged for all those years?"

"Kristen," he waved his hand out in frustration and sadly shook his head. "The only thing I know is what is common knowledge."

"Which is more than I know," she reminded him. "Please tell me."

He took a deep breath and sat back from the table. "Your father and his father, your paternal grandfather, had a terrible argument nearly thirty years ago, and immediately following the altercation your father left Greece, never to return again. Your aunt only discovered your father's whereabouts after. . . the events of your wedding made the papers."

"But how?" she shook her head, confused.

"Your name. Evidently your father anglicized his name after coming to live here. That's why your aunt couldn't locate him. But when she saw your name in the paper she put two and two together and came up with your father."

She shook her head. She was still confused. "I don't understand."

Paul patiently explained. "Your name 'King' is the exact translation of your Greek name 'Vasilias.' And your first name is a derivative of your grandmother's name, 'Christina.' It's the tradition in Greece to name children after grandparents."

She blinked and threw up her hands in total amazement, "I don't believe it. . .I was named for my grandmother. . .and never knew it. . ."

"It does seem unbelievable," he agreed.

Kristen shook her head. She was bewildered. It didn't fit with her father's character at all. "I just don't understand. My father was a wonderful man. I can't believe that he would cut himself off from his sister for all those years because of an argument he had with his father. I can't even remember my father arguing with anyone."

"And the same goes for Aphrodite," he said in defense of his nona. "She can be formidable, particularly in the business world," he admitted, "but she's a very lovely lady."

They sat in silence for several moments. The movements in the restaurant and the beat of the city outside ticked off the passing of time as Kristen tried to assimilate all that she had just learned.

"I wish I had the knowledge to tell you all that you want to know about the estrangement between your aunt and your father," Paul interrupted her thoughts, "but I'm afraid that I'm not privy to that information." His lips twisted at the corners. "It's a mystery to me, the one thing that Nona won't talk to me about." He paused. "But, maybe she'll tell you. Please come to Athens."

She smiled, a smile of wonder. "You know. . .it's kind of funny. . .so much has been pointing me in that direction."

Now it was his turn to be confused. "What do you mean?"

"Well. . .a really close friend of mine is an archaeologist living in Athens for the next several years, and a girl I went to university with has recently married a Greek man and is living in the Peloponnese. She's asked me to visit her several times."

"That's amazing," he agreed and then, lowering his voice, he referred to their earlier conversation. "Sounds like this is the path you are meant to follow, Kristen."

She looked into his dark eyes and nodded. "I think you may be right." She glanced down at her gold watch. It had been over an hour since she'd left the hotel. "I have to get back." She stood, and opening her purse, removed a business card and extended it to him. "Call me tomorrow, and I'll let you know when and if I can get away."

Paul nodded and reaching for the card, said, "Thank you, Kristen. You will make an old lady very happy."

They stood looking at one another for a long moment knowing that they would make themselves happy as well.

Finally, Paul leaned over and kissed Kristen in the European fashion of a kiss on either side of the face. The mild roughness of his smoothly shaven face rubbed against the smoothness of her's. Kristen closed her eyes and savored the moment. He smelled so good, so masculine and good.

"Let me see you back to the hotel," he offered, his voice deep with emotion.

Kristen shook her head. "I'd like to see myself back if you don't mind." She had a great deal to think over and she needed those few moments to be alone. On top of thoughts about her aunt, she needed to think about her feelings for this man, who she was now quite sure was meant to be in her life for more than just one afternoon.

He smiled and stood back for her to pass. "I understand."

She smiled up at him and then turning, walked toward the door.

As she went, Paul noticed that the back of her neck, which he had thought so vulnerable when he first saw her, was now covered with a few wisps of windblown hair. It seemed less vulnerable to him now, safer somehow, and he was glad. Glad mostly to know that he might have the chance to get to know her, to care for her, to protect her from the hurts of the world. It was something that he wanted to do, something that he wanted to do very badly.

four

Kristen stepped from her glass-enclosed shower stall that evening onto the white ceramic floor, feeling refreshed and revitalized. The chocolate cake she'd put in the oven before her shower tantalized her with its aroma as it wafted in through the open door of her bedroom and into the connecting bathroom.

Wrapping her head in a pink velour towel, she quickly rubbed her body dry with a matching one and reached for a red cotton T-shirt that had Williamsburg, Virginia, emblazoned across the front of it, and a pair of jean shorts to go with it.

Even though it was her birthday, Kristen didn't dress up, as she was planning on spending the evening much as she passed every night. Alone.

Padding through her flowery bedroom with its large brass bed, into the living area, she pulled the towel from her head and absently rubbed the tangled strands of her dark hair, made darker now by being wet. She unlocked the sliding glass door, and using her hip, pushed open the door which commanded an eye-riveting ocean view.

A deep, contented sigh escaped her body as she appreciated the beauty spread out before her. She closed her eyes and inhaled deeply from the sweetness of the ocean air. The wind was still blowing hard and whipped the salt spray from the foaming, churning ocean up to touch her skin, tingling it.

She walked forward to the wooden planter that ran along the length of the deck's railing, and bending, plucked a dried leaf from a red geranium plant.

Crushing the leaf in her fingers, Kristen held the grainy pieces up over the wooden railing and let the wind pick them up to carry them far away across the mighty sea and she thought how those bits were just like her. She had been as dried out as that leaf after her husband's duplicity and death, but because of another man she was learning to be a person who could risk feeling, and a person who could risk crossing the ocean to meet her unknown aunt and to search for that Unknown, Something More that she knew was missing in her life.

Abruptly, she wiped her hand against her shorts, and tossing the wet towel across a deck chair to let it air dry, Kristen turned away from the view that had sold her the house, and strode purposefully back into the living room intending to go straight to the bathroom in order to comb out her tangled hair. But the aroma of the chocolate cake baking in the oven made her stop. It made her house smell yummy and cozy like a family home would.

And, it reminded her unmercifully of her parents.

Taking a deep, steadying breath, Kristen resolved not to let herself get maudlin. She wouldn't let it happen.

Not today. Too many wonderful things had happened today and she knew that her parents wouldn't want her to feel sad on this, her first birthday without them.

She reached for the gold chain around her neck which glistened from its recent wash and absently rubbed it between her fingers. No. . .as much as she missed her parents, she wouldn't let herself feel sad today and she resolved to decorate her cake with icing and candles in keeping with their family tradition. The only thing was. . .her father had always iced her cake.

Squaring her shoulders, Kristen decided to leave those thoughts behind and was about to continue on her way to the bathroom, when from the corner of her eye, a movement captured her attention. Fluttering above her coffee table around her little statue of the *Youth of Antikythera* was a beautiful yellow butterfly.

Kristen turned to it slowly, not wanting to scare it away, and with cupped hands, walked toward it with the hope that the elegant insect would land within them. But the butterfly did not. Instead it chose to land on the long, straight, classical nose of *The Youth*.

Kristen laughed softly, sounding a bit like fine crystal tinkling in the wind. "Little butterfly, I see that you like my little statue, too."

As if in answer, the butterfly rose in flight and fluttered gracefully around the twelve-inch statue.

"I hope I didn't flutter around the 'Man from Greece' like that today," Kristen laughingly sang out and watched as the butterfly winged its way off toward the open door to the flowers beyond.

With the rays of the sun touching the tips of its wings, it was as golden as Paul Andrakos's thick hair, and Kristen thought how it seemed to gleam its joy in being free and alive. And she couldn't help but think that that was exactly how Paul had made her feel today—free and alive, golden and warm.

As the graceful butterfly disappeared from sight somewhere over the bent sea pines, Kristen turned back to the statue on the glass-topped table. Plopping herself down on the floral sofa before it, she said, "Well, little *Youth*, I guess it's just you and me again."

She twisted her head like an artist sizing up a picture. "Seeing you close at hand, I have to admit that Paul Andrakos's hair isn't nearly as curly as yours. His is wavy. And his lips seem more straight than yours and, more, well. . ." Kristen tipped her head from side to side trying to decide, "older." She finally decided that age was the difference.

"You are a youth after all, and he is a man. But except for your curly hair, if you were twenty years older, and alive, of course, you would be identical," she said and hopped up from the sofa. "I'm going to get a glass of milk. What shall I get for you, my quiet little one?" Kristen asked over her shoulder as she walked around the bar that divided the two rooms. "Perhaps a rag to wipe the dust from your handsome face?"

Reaching into the refrigerator, Kristen continued her one-sided dialogue. "Don't feel bad, little friend, but I think that I would much prefer the company of the 'Man from Greece' to yours tonight," she mused, and started to pour milk into a long-stemmed crystal wine glass. "And the nice thing is, I even think that I could handle it."

The doorbell chimed. Startled, Kristen slopped milk onto the counter. Leaving her glass in a puddle of white, she turned and walked hesitantly back into the living room toward the front door.

About five feet in front of it, she stopped, and rubbing her suddenly clammy hands against her shorts, she eyed the door skeptically, as if it hid a monster behind it.

Except for Lottie, and her Uncle George when he'd been in town, Kristen hadn't had anyone else over to her house in the months that she'd lived there. It had been her refuge from the world, her place of healing, and acting in a way that was alien to her personality, that had been outgoing and sociable before Ted, Kristen had in fact become a recluse.

The doorbell chimed again, this time sounding impatient to be kept waiting.

"This is ridiculous," Kristen whispered, walking toward the door, finally realizing that her Uncle George had probably sent her flowers for her birthday.

Lifting her eyes toward the little pinpoint of light filtering in through the peephole, Kristen spied the handsome face of Paul Andrakos on the other side. She jumped back as if she had been zapped by a laser beam!

"I don't believe it!" she whispered and quickly ran her fingers through her uncombed hair.

"Kristen?" She heard his deep voice call through the wood of the door. That melodious voice, that magical voice.

She glanced back at her little statue. It seemed to be grinning now.

"Well, little *Youth*, I think I'm about to receive my wish. The 'Man from Greece' is here!" Deciding that nothing else mattered other than seeing Paul Andrakos again, not her uncombed hair nor even her casual dress, Kristen slid the lock on the door, and couldn't help but smile at the thought that it was symbolic of sliding open her heart, too. She swung the door wide without hesitation.

"Paul! What a wonderful surprise!" she exclaimed and meant it.

"I hope you don't mind my just dropping in on you like this, but—" from behind his back he whooshed a dozen full-bloomed yellow roses set among innumerable buds, "it is your birthday."

"Oh!" She reached for the flowers, and cradling them in her arms, bent her head to inhale their clean honest fragrance. "Oh, Paul, they're beautiful! What a lovely surprise!"

She had no way of knowing how absolutely refreshing she appeared to him. Her hair in a damp tangle around her shoulders and her face clean of all makeup was as truthful an account of womanhood that Paul could ever remember seeing. She was beautiful but her physical beauty was only part of what he felt for her. He loved the way she opened the door to him even though she obviously wasn't dressed to have guests, and he loved the truthfulness that he read in her eyes every time she looked at him.

"When I selected them at the florist I intended to have them delivered, but then I got this crazy idea to bring them myself," he explained his appearance, but left off the jealousy he felt over thinking that an unknown deliveryman might tread where he, by convention, really should not have.

"I'm so glad you did."

"But just pretend that I'm the deliveryman. I'll be on my way now. I'm sure that you have plans for the night," he said and started to back away, all the while hoping that she would stop him. He felt like a lovesick adolescent.

"No!" she quickly shouted out. She didn't want him leaving. "I mean, I don't have any plans and I would love for you to come in."

"Are you sure?" He wanted to come in and spend the evening with her more than anything.

"Yes. I mean," she licked her lips, "we have things to discuss, and I have a cake in the oven. . . ." That wasn't what she wanted to say, but, if it kept him with her, she would say almost anything. "Do come in." She stepped to the side and motioned for him to enter.

He nodded and stepped past her. "The cake smells delicious."

"It will be ready soon." She looked down at her clothes and touched her tangled hair. She could feel his gaze sweep over her. If she were a person who could blush, she was sure that she would have then.

"I'll just be a moment while I change." Kristen placed the roses on the hall table. "Please, make yourself at home." She motioned toward the living room before turning on her bare feet to retreat to the bedroom.

As she closed the door to her bedroom, she saw Paul walk into her living room and she really couldn't believe that he was in her house, seeing her things. She knew that after tonight her home would never be quite the same, *but in a good way,* she thought, as a smile covered her whole face.

With super speed, Kristen tore off her shorts and T-shirt and selected from her closet a skirt with tropical flowers on it and a matching silk blouse which she had bought on an impulse two weeks ago but hadn't worn because of a lack of occasion. It was too feminine for the office, but perfect for tonight. She splashed on some mild perfume, whisked on a bit of rouge and a splash of lipstick. Her hair was practically dry so she brushed it until her comb could go through the thick strands, added a leather hairband, and donning her skirt and blouse and a pair of white pumps, quickly went back into the living room.

She couldn't help laughing softly when she saw Paul holding her little statue. He looked up at her and smiled. If he had thought that she looked sophisticatedly attractive at lunch and wholesomely honest just earlier, he now thought she looked alluringly beautiful. He liked Kristen in every mode.

She saw Paul's appreciation and rejoiced in it. She had dressed for him right now and acknowledged to herself that it felt good to dress for a man once again. Meeting Paul was changing her back into the person she used to be before life took so many unpleasant turns.

He held up the statue. "When I was younger, my nona used to tease me and tell me that I could have been the model for this guy." He looked at the statue and frowned. "But I can't see the resemblance. Can you?" he asked and Kristen had the distinct impression that he didn't like the idea.

"Perhaps when you were younger you did look similar," she offered diplomatically.

Paul held it in front of him, still frowning. "His hair is too wavy and—"

"—he's very handsome, Paul." Kristen inserted.

"You think so?"

"Definitely."

"So," his dark eyes deepened and crinkled in the corners. "Does that mean you think that I am handsome?" Paul motioned toward the statue before he again put it in its place on the table.

"Paul?" she tilted her head over her right shoulder as she walked toward the kitchen, intending to test her cake to see if it was done, "you surely can't be fishing for a compliment?"

"I can."

She laughed and he liked the free way it sounded. In her home, Kristen was different, in a nicer, freer way, and he was very glad that he'd had the nerve to deliver the flowers himself. "Then, yes," she answered from the kitchen as he came to stand in the entranceway, "as you undoubtedly know, you are handsome." Kristen laughed again as she pulled a toothpick from its holder in order to check the cake and couldn't help adding impishly, "and I agree with your godmother, your nona, you do look like you were the model for that statue."

Taking the toothpick from her hand, Paul chuckled, a deep and comfortable sound to her ears. "May I check the cake?" he motioned toward the oven.

With a tilt of her head, Kristen stepped out of the way as he opened the oven door.

"Ummm, smells great!" He tested the cake. "And I'd say it's done, too," he pronounced, and reaching for her yellow potholders, removed the cake from the oven.

"You're very handy in a kitchen," Kristen commented, "especially. . .for a model of a statue," she teased. But at the challenging look that came into his eyes, she quickly held up her hand in truce and said, "I'm sorry, I shouldn't have started that again. I'll only say one last thing about the statue and then I'll leave the subject alone."

"And that is?" he prompted, understanding she was up to something.

"And that is. . ." she pinched a piece of cake from the top and blew on it before touching the tip of her tongue to it. "I was thinking maybe we could go to the National Archaeological Museum of Greece and see the real statue sometime, together?"

"Kristen?" he waited without seeming to take a breath and the importance he placed on her answer impressed her and made Kristen feel wonderful.

She nodded her head affirmatively. "As of tomorrow afternoon, I'm on holiday for a month, and free to leave for Athens whenever you say the word."

"Kristen," he repeated and moved toward her and as his arms wrapped around her, she closed her eyes and savored the moment. It felt so right and so good to be held by a man after so long, but as Kristen rested her head against Paul's chest and smelled the essence of him, she knew that it was this man, and this man alone, whom she had only met this day, with whom it felt so right.

"I'm so glad." His voice was husky and deep, and very, very soft.

"Me, too," she looked up to his face and let her eyes roam around the classical planes of it before speaking. "I can't wait to meet my aunt, and—"

"—and," he prompted, following her eyes with his as they traveled his face.

". . .and," she licked her lips before stepping back from him and whispering, "maybe, maybe we can start searching for that Unknown, Something More, together?"

He smiled a deep, warm smile that was glad for this woman

who wanted more from a relationship than the superficial goals advertised so expertly throughout the world today. "I'd like nothing more, Kristen, than to go on that search together."

Paul didn't touch her again, but Kristen felt as though he had. There was a closeness growing between them that transcended the physical. Like the wind, it seemed to wrap around them and touch them, and weave them together with its invisible threads. "But. . .where do we start?" she asked.

He was unsure but he let common sense prevail. "Well, every search has a beginning, a path to follow. We just have to find that beginning and take it."

The doorbell rang, startling them both.

"I wonder who that could be?" Kristen asked as she walked toward the front door. Since Paul was with her she felt safe, so she didn't even bother to look through the peephole. She opened the door to a deliveryman who gave her a rather large package. She signed for it and kicking the door shut, read the postmark and exclaimed, "It's from my friend, Lottie, the archaeologist who is living in Athens!"

"Must be a birthday gift," Paul commented.

Running into the kitchen to get her scissors, Kristen nodded excitedly. "Last year she gave me the little statue." She ran back into the living room and sitting on the sofa, stared at the package for a moment before attacking the string with the scissors.

He laughed. "Wow, you do like opening packages!"

She laughed with him and nodded, unashamed, "I really do!" She tore at the brown paper until two gayly-wrapped packages appeared.

Paul picked up one of them and weighed it in his hands. "Feels like a book."

Kristen held the other one and nodded, "This one too. Oh, I love books and I imagine they must have something to do with Greece! Isn't that amazing, since I am going there soon!" She looked up at Paul, her eyes sparkling.

Paul laughed at her enthusiasm and handed her the package he held. "Quite amazing. Now why don't you open one and see exactly what it is."

Kristen sighed excitedly and looked from one to the other. "Yes, but which one should I open first?"

Paul pointed to one. "This one."

"Why this one and not that one?" She queried playfully.

"Because it says," he read the words written in among the stripes of the paper, " 'Kristen, please open this package first.' "

Kristen laughed and looked where Paul pointed. "Oh, I didn't see that!" She smiled up at him, then slipping her finger behind the taped end she carefully removed the wrapping. Flipping the book over, Kristen and Paul both gasped when they saw the book it was.

"A Bible. . ." Kristen whispered and looked up at Paul.

"THE HOLY BIBLE," Paul read the words emblazoned in gold across the brown leather.

And they looked at one another in amazement.

five

"No one has ever given me a Bible before," Kristen whispered and ran her fingertips over the smoothness of the gold lettering.

Paul shook his head. He was amazed by the gift. "Me neither."

With innate reverence, Kristen opened the book and read out loud the long inscription her friend had made.

> *To Kristen on her Birthday,*
> *The reading of this book has taught me that there is a birth even greater than the one you experienced twenty-eight years ago today.*
> *It is the birth into God's kingdom which our Lord Jesus describes so nicely to Nicodemus in the third chapter of the Book of John and which I have been born into since coming to this ancient city of Athens.*
> *I thought Athens was going to be good for my career; it has ended up being good for much, much more. No one ever knows what the future holds but I do know now that this book is the key to life because it comes from God. In it, he talks to us all—a gift to be cherished.*
> *There is a verse in the book of Psalms which sums up what this book has come to mean to me and which I hope comes to mean as much to you, Kristen.*
> *"Your word is a lamp to my feet and a light for my path."*
> *I hope your "path" brings you to Athens so that I may show you this wonderful city and even more, tell you in person about the wonderful knowledge, the*

wonderful news I have learned since coming here.
> *Your Friend,*
> *Lottie*

Kristen stopped reading and slowly turned to Paul. "I have goosebumps breaking out on my arms. Can you believe the coincidence of it all?"

Paul took a deep breath and reaching for Kristen's arm, rubbed the goosebumps that had indeed appeared there. "I've never put much stock in coincidence, Kristen," he paused. "There's a power much greater than chance working here."

She slowly nodded her head and whispered, "You feel it too?"

"I feel it." He let go of her arm and reached for the book. "And I think we have been given our starting place in our search for that Something More."

She looked back down at the book. "I know some of the Bible stories but. . .I don't even know how to read this book."

"Well. . .I guess as with anything. . .you start at the beginning."

He pointed at the other package which still awaited opening. "Maybe that book will help."

Kristen turned to look at the package that remained unopened and nodding, reached for it. She was still excited but in a much deeper, more mature way that somehow knew that this moment of discovery was monumental to her life, to Paul's life. She slipped off the bright wrapping paper and turning over the book, found that it was a Bible Handbook and Concordance. She flipped through its pages. "I guess it helps us to read the Bible. Look," she pointed out the headings, "it goes along with the chapters in the Bible. . .Genesis, Exodus . . .all of them."

He frowned, remembering something. "But they aren't called 'chapters,' they're different Books that make up the Bible. The Book of Genesis, The Book of Exodus, etc. . . ."

She looked at him surprised. "You seem to know quite a bit

more than I do."

"The Christian religion is a part of the Greek school curriculum," he smiled wryly, "I guess something had to sink in." He reached for the book and as she gave it to him a card fell out of the pages. Picking it up off the floor he handed it to her. "I have a feeling your friend has a few suggestions."

Kristen laughingly replied, "That sounds like Lottie!" Opening the envelope, Kristen removed a card which had a picture of the city of Athens on its front. "Oh, Paul, look!" she pointed out the picture. "It's your city! Can you see where you live?"

He took the card and pointed to where the cliffs of the butte-shaped Acropolis, the ancient High City which had so many monumental buildings from Greece's golden past sitting upon it, including the world famous Parthenon, the temple that was built to honor the Greek god Athena, and said, "I've recently refurbished a neoclassical home in Anafiotika."

"Anafiotika. . ." she repeated the unusual name.

"It's part of the old town, built on the northeastern slopes below the Acropolis. My house is somewhere around here."

"Paul! I had no idea!" But she wasn't surprised to learn that he lived in the historical area. Somehow all that was modern and chrome didn't suit his personality. "It must be wonderful!" She scrutinized the card.

"Can you see your house?"

He chuckled and tilted his head upward in the Greek expression for no. "I think it would take a magnifying glass to find it."

"It must be beautiful there," she said almost dreamily.

"It's home," he replied simply.

"I guess you can run up to the Acropolis anytime you want to."

He chuckled again. "Well—as a matter of fact—I do jog around its perimeters whenever there aren't too many tourists and whenever I have time, which unfortunately isn't often enough. Although I haven't been up to the Acropolis itself in years." He laughed. "I think the last time was on a high school field trip."

Kristen shook her head. "Imagine going on a school field trip to the Acropolis of Athens. . ."

He smiled and pointed to the card again. "This picture was taken from the mountain behind your aunt's—and your father's—and your—ancestral home."

Kristen shook her head. "It's beautiful. . .I can't believe this is where my father grew up and where my aunt is today. . ."

"And where you will be in a couple of days," he reminded her gently.

She nodded almost in awe. "And where I will be in a couple of days. . ."

She sat, entranced by the picture for a few moments until Paul said with good-natured impatience, "Come on. . .read what Lottie has to say."

She smiled up at him and opened the card. "I think you are as excited as I am."

"Maybe even more," he agreed. His tone was serious. "I feel as though the search that I have wanted to go on for so long is about to begin and it's amazing to think that its start is coming from a friend of yours who now lives in my city."

"It's like. . .something is weaving the fabric of our lives together. . ." she stopped and looked down at the card in her hand, suddenly embarrassed.

He gently touched her cheek with his thumb, silently asking her to look at him and his voice was deep with emotion as he spoke, "Perhaps. . .that Something More that we are looking for. . .?"

She bit her lower lip and nodded, "Perhaps. . ." she agreed and started to read what Lottie wrote.

> *Dear Kristen,*
> *As you might know, Athens is a Biblical city.*

Kristen looked over at Paul and frowned. "I didn't know that Athens was a Biblical city."

He nodded. "Many of the first Christians visited there. . ."

among them St. Paul. It's written about it in the Bible some-where."

Kristen shook her head in wonder before continuing to read.

> *I think this fact has made Athens extra special to me. . .it certainly has inspired me as I discover the joys of being a new Christian in this ancient city.*
> *The Bible Handbook and Concordance will help you as you read the Bible. The Handbook helps to explain the setting, mood, and history of what you might be reading and the concordance is there to help you locate certain subjects. Let's say you want to find all the verses in the Bible that have the word* path *in them. Look up* path *and you will find them plus their location in the Bible.*
> *Please come and visit me soon.*
>
> *Happy Birthday,*
Lottie

Kristen fell silent. Her thumb rubbed lovingly over the words that her friend had cared enough to write to her.

"Path. . ." Paul spoke the word into the wondrous silence that surrounded them.

Kristen nodded and looked up at Paul. "Path. . .my path. . . your path. . ." She took a deep breath and unfolding herself from the soft cushions of the sofa, walked over to the window to gaze out at the setting sun. It hung over the churning ocean, like a lone Christmas tree ornament which someone had neglected to remove from the tree.

"You know. . ." she began softly, "I think that I have always believed in the God of my ancestors. It's traditional," she played with the chain around her neck. "But. . ." she turned back to Paul, "He has always seemed so remote, so unknown to me." She shrugged her shoulders, confirming the vulnerability Paul had thought to be hers when he first met her.

Rising, he walked over to the window to stand next to her.

"I think I know what you mean."

She shook her head and turned to him. "No. . .what I mean is. . .I think that I have always blamed God for that. . .for the fact that He's unknown and remote to me. . .but I'm beginning to realize that it's my fault," she touched her palm to her chest, "my fault. . ." she repeated, "that I haven't known Him better." She walked over to pick up the brand new Bible from the table where it lay so quietly, so unassumingly, and yet, so forcefully. "How can I blame God for not knowing Him when I haven't even read this book which is all about Him?"

Paul smiled wryly, guiltily. "I see what you mean. I think it's something many of us are guilty of in this day and age."

"Well. . .it's going to change for me." She plopped down on the sofa and with determination, seemed ready to start reading the Bible then and there. "I'm going to read this book and see if it has some of the answers that I'm looking for."

Paul sat down next to her. "Good idea, but. . ." he touched her chin and turning her face to his, smiled that dazzling smile which made Kristen's insides turn upside down. "Do you suppose I could have a piece of that birthday cake before you start?" he asked. "It is rather a long book."

She laughed softly. "Oh, Paul. I'm sorry." She put the Bible on the coffee table and hopping up from the sofa, walked toward the kitchen for the cake. "I have to decorate it first," she called back over her shoulder.

"What? Decorate your own birthday cake?" he questioned in mock horror, and standing, moved toward her just as the phone rang out insistently. "You answer that noisy machine and let me," he bounced his fingers against his chest, "decorate your cake."

She eyed him dubiously as the phone continued its demanding ring.

"Do you know how?"

With mock exasperation, he asked, "Why is it that women always think men are so incapable in the kitchen?" He laughed and pushed her in the direction of the crying phone.

She paused and pensively replied, "Actually, I don't. My

father was a whiz in the kitchen. In fact. . .he always made and decorated my birthday cakes. . .always. . ." she finished on a sad note.

Paul felt her pain at not having her parents with her this year on her birthday and a part of him wanted to forget the cake, forget the ringing phone and go to her, wrapping her safely in the protection of his arms. But he knew that in the long run that action would only make things worse. Instead, he nodded toward the phone. "Whoever is calling you is going to hang up soon," he reminded her softly. The caring he felt was in his tone.

She nodded and as Paul continued into the kitchen she reached for the phone.

Paul found the icing supplies on the counter and began to ice the cake. He didn't mean to eavesdrop on Kristen's conversation, but with only a shuttered breakfast bar separating him from the living room, he couldn't help but overhear every word she said.

"Uncle George! What a nice surprise!" The pleasure in her voice was obvious but Paul frowned at her use of the title. He didn't think that she had any other living relatives, not even on her mother's side, and he wondered who this "Uncle" George could be.

"You will! Tomorrow night?" A pause. "That's great. And don't worry that you couldn't surprise me today, I've already had enough surprises for today. . ." A pause. "Well. . .a man from Greece came today. . .from my aunt. . .she wants me to come and visit her!" She spoke excitedly but from the subdued sound of her voice when she spoke again, Paul was sure that this "Uncle" George wasn't too pleased with her news.

"No. . .I'm fine. . .and Uncle George. . .I'm glad. . .please be glad for me. . .you can meet him tomorrow night and see for yourself."

There was another long pause before Kristen again spoke words of reassurance. She seemed to be cutting her "uncle" off firmly but nicely. "—Uncle George. . .don't worry. . ." A pause. "Because my aunt's been sick," she explained. "Well

. . .I'm glad that you're coming tomorrow so that you can meet him and see for yourself. Don't worry. . .I'm a big girl now. . ." She paused and Paul could tell from her voice that she was smiling into the phone. "I love you too. . .thanks for calling. . .bye. . ." She hung up the phone just as Paul put the finishing touches on icing the cake.

Kristen strode into the kitchen and stood leaning against the door frame. "I hope you can come over tomorrow evening. A very dear friend is going to come to wish me happy birthday and I'd like for you to meet one another."

His back to her, Paul replied truthfully about what he had overheard, "I don't think your 'Uncle' George is too pleased to hear that I'm here."

She arched her brows at Paul's use of her caller's name and looking at her over his shoulder, he explained, "Sorry, but I couldn't help overhearing."

"No. . .it's okay. If I had wanted privacy, I would have gone into my bedroom." She wiped up the milk she'd spilled earlier and opened the cupboard for two dessert plates. "Uncle George is a bit protective of me."

"Are you related somehow?"

As she placed the bone china plates on the counter she shook her head. "No. . .as I said earlier today. . .I don't have any blood relatives other than my aunt. Uncle George was a longtime friend of my parents. . .they were like siblings . . .since they died. . .he has kind of watched over me."

"Sounds like a nice man."

"He is. I love him like, like. . ." she fished around for a good way to describe her feelings for the older man and finally settled on the most obvious analogy, "a beloved uncle. I've known him all my life."

"And he's coming tomorrow night?"

She dipped the tip of her finger into what was left of the chocolate icing and licked it clean before explaining. "He lives in Virginia, in Richmond, where I used to live. He had planned on surprising me tonight. . .but he was unable to get away."

Paul placed the icing knife in the sink with a *plonk* and

picking up the tubes of decorative icing and birthday candles said, "Well, I'm glad that I'll have the chance to meet him. But for now," he nudged her in the direction of the living room, "let me finish my job so we can eat this delicious-smelling cake."

"Can't I watch?" she asked impishly over her shoulder as she walked out of the kitchen.

"No way. . .it has to be a surprise. Now out!"

As she padded into the living room Kristen laughed, a happy, gay sound that only went a fragment of the way in telling how happy she really was that Paul had come to her house that night.

She couldn't help but think how differently the evening had turned out because of this man who had come from her aunt. Without him, she would have been alone and sad. With him, she wasn't sad and she wasn't alone.

Sitting down on the sofa, she reached forward and picked up the books Lottie had sent to her. She held both of them on her lap and inhaled the lovely scent that could only belong to new books. She listened to the sound of Paul whistling "Happy Birthday" as he worked in the kitchen. She watched the curtains as they danced to the beat of the strong wind blowing off the Pacific and she knew that she hadn't been happier in a very long time, in a *very, very* long time. The day had turned and twisted in such different directions from that which she had thought it would carry her when she had awoken to her birthday all alone that morning.

She put the Bible down and on a sudden impulse, leafed through the concordance in search for the word *path*. When she found it, she was surprised to see so many verses which included the word, and a little bit daunted. Since she wasn't sure where to start searching she started with the first one.

She read out loud, " 'Ps 16:11 known to me the p'. . .must be path. . .'of life'."

Picking up the Bible, she looked through the index, discovered that 'Ps' stood for the Book of Psalms, found the page number for the beginning of the Book, turned to it, and from there turned the pages until she found the sixteenth chapter and then the eleventh verse. Her eyes lit up when she saw that she had found the correct verse.

She read, "You have made known to me the path of life. . ." She lifted her eyes to the mighty Pacific outside her window that was still visible in the lingering light of an already setting sun. But Kristen didn't see its beauty. Instead, the words she had just read made her see something within herself that was even more wondrous and mighty than the ocean beyond her window.

She looked back down at the book and slowly repeated the words, "You have made known to me the path of life. . .the path of life. . ." And she thought how magnificent it was that there was indeed a "path of life" and how it was something that could be made known to her.

"Are you ready?" Paul's voice boomed out from the kitchen, startling her.

Kristen wanted to share what she had just discovered with Paul, so she was careful to leave the Bible opened as she put it down on the coffee table before her. "I'm ready," she returned and as she smoothed out the folds of her skirt, thought that it was wonderful to feel happy again.

"Then here I come." He walked into the living room whistling "Happy Birthday" and holding the cake, now ablaze with candles, in front of him.

She laughed, delighted that he had filled it with twenty-eight candles instead of a token few. "Wow! It looks like a bonfire!"

"Well it just might become one if you don't hurry and blow them out," he admonished with a smile and placed the cake on the table before her. "*Hronia Polla*, Kristen. . ." he spoke the Greek birthday wish meaning "Many Years" which he'd written on her cake and she sucked in her breath when she saw the Greek letters. "It means—"

"Oh Paul. . ." she cut him off and her eyes, reflecting the light of her twenty-eight birthday candles, glistened with tears. "I know what '*Hronia Polla*' means. . ."

"Kristen—?" He questioned softly, concerned by the tears.

She touched the corner of her eyes with a birthday napkin and smiled, a sweet smile which held gladness in it. "Don't worry. . .these are tears of happiness. I thought I'd never see nor hear those words again," she paused and then explained. "You see. . .my father always wrote them on my birthday cakes. Ever since I was a little girl. . .they're practically the only Greek words I know and they're very special to me."

Happiness filled him and he knew then that the best way for him to be happy was to always be able to make this woman happy.

Touching her shoulder in gentle understanding, he nodded toward the cake. "You'd better blow the candles out."

She squeezed her eyes shut and, looking to Paul like a little girl who was wishing with all her heart for her birthday wish to come true, opened her eyes and blew all the candles out at the same moment.

Paul clapped. "Bravo, Kristen. . .now your wish will come true."

"I hope so," she whispered and looked at him in a way that made him feel as though he was a part of that wish. "But for the first time," she continued, "my wish was more like a prayer."

"A prayer?" he questioned. That surprised him.

She reached for the Bible as he sat down next to her. "Look what I just discovered." She pointed out the verse in the sixteenth chapter of Psalms.

"'You have made known to me the" he paused as he silently read the next words before speaking them out loud, "path of life. . .'" He turned amazed eyes toward Kristen.

She nodded. "See. . .my birthday wish—prayer—is that the 'You' in that verse makes known to me the path of my life and along that 'path' I hope that I can discover who exactly the 'You' is."

He nodded and not wanting to discourage her, but also not wanting her to be disappointed, felt that he had to remind her of a simple truth. "You know, sometimes our paths go in

ways we least expect them to go and sometimes in ways we
prefer them not to go."

"Don't I know that," she expounded, that old familiar bitterness creeping into her voice. "I thought that I would be happily married at this point in my life, maybe even a mother who
could take her children to visit their grandparents. Instead, I'm
legally a widow to a man who only meant to use me," she
paused and breathed out in disgust, "or, I should say, use my
money—and even if I had children, my parents aren't living
anymore to go and visit."

"Kristen," he took her hand in his and gently squeezed it.
That her husband had married her for her money was news to
him and something that explained a lot about her and—it was
something to which he could relate. It made him want to protect her more. If he thought that he had to go slow and easy
with her before, he was now certain of it. She had had too
many hurts in her life and he wanted to do everything in his
power to make sure that she wasn't hurt again.

An amazed frown drew his brows together in a straight line
as it occurred to him that he felt this way because he loved
her. He loved her. . .as he had never loved nor would ever
love. . .again. . .and he knew that he had loved her from practically the first moment he saw her.

She watched him frown and totally misreading his expression, was immediately disgusted with herself for letting him
see her bitterness over the events in her life. She had already
told him how confused she was about things. . .did she have
to add bitterness to the list? Wishing she had kept her mouth
shut, she withdrew her hand from his and asked brightly, too
brightly, "How about a slice of cake?"

Still amazed by his thought, Paul absently nodded and
Kristen escaped into the kitchen for plates and silverware and
to regain her equilibrium.

Resting her forehead against the cupboard, Kristen squeezed
her eyes shut and admonished herself for letting her bitterness
over her disastrous marriage and her parents' deaths mar the
evening. She didn't understand how it had happened but she

knew that her feelings for Paul were running true and deep and getting deeper by the moment. She was looking forward to traveling to Greece to meet her aunt but somehow, in the course of the last few hours, she knew that it had become even more important for her to go to Greece in order to be with Paul. She hardly knew him and yet, somehow she felt that she knew him better than anyone else in the world. Her soul responded to his, and from somewhere the expression "soulmate" found its way into Kristen's brain and she smiled. For that was what Paul had become to her, and a part of her, a part that had been wounded and left bleeding for far too long, was mending and trusting and beginning to. . .love again.

That thought shocked Kristen and she banged her head lightly against the cupboard.

"Do you need some help in there?" Paul called out, startling her.

"No. I'm coming." But she was shocked by her thoughts. *Do I truly love Paul Andrakos?* she wondered as she absently rubbed her head and then quickly gathered napkins and plates and silverware onto a serving tray. And how could it have happened so suddenly? Was it possible to fall in love with a man in only a few hours?

Squaring her shoulders, she walked back into the living room with the tray and sat next to Paul. She was aware of him in a way that was different from before, in a way that was both frightening and thrilling, and made her feel shy, like an adolescent. She was glad to have something to do with her hands and after removing the candles she sliced two big pieces of cake, one for each of them.

As she handed a plate to Paul she whispered, "Paul. . .I'm sorry for my outburst." She shrugged her shoulders, looking very vulnerable to Paul as she did so. "I guess. . .sometimes the anger I feel over how things have turned out. . ." her voice trailed off.

Putting his plate down, Paul reached for her hand, quieting her with his touch. "Kristen, no. . .don't ever apologize for being honest with me."

She shrugged her shoulders again, making Paul ache over her vulnerability. "It's just that. . .I don't want you to think that I'm this bitter person who is obsessed with the past and angry all the time and confused the rest of the time."

Paul silenced her by lightly touching his finger to her lips. Her eyes turned to his and the agitation she had felt was squelched by what she saw written in the depths of his dark, warm eyes.

Slowly his mouth moved and the words which he spoke were like a soothing balm to her soul. "What I think about you is that you are lovely. . .both inside and out. We've only met this day but I feel as though I have known you forever."

"Paul. . ." She reached out and rubbed his face with her hand, a light touch of caring that made Paul, in spite of his resolve to go slow with her, unable to do so.

"Dear Kristen," he placed his hand over hers and the sounds of the deepening night, the breaking surf, the wind above it, their breath and pulse beats all combined to produce a symphony of sound, a symphony of life, that drew them together. "Dear Kristen. . ." he repeated, "I never believed in love at first sight. . .until now. . ."

"Paul. . ." she whispered his name in wonder that he could possibly feel for her. . .what she knew she felt for him. Her hand turned to hold his and he grasped her smaller one between both of his, gently bringing her closer to him.

His eyes spoke the words a moment before his mouth and Kristen had no doubts that they both spoke the truth, "Darling Kristen. . .as amazing as it might seem—I am falling in love with you. . ."

Her eyes answered him before her mouth, but Paul too knew that they both spoke the truth, "And. . .I. . .am falling in love with you. . .Paul. . ."

And their vow was sealed by a kiss, their first kiss. It was a simple kiss of love, of meaning, of two souls who had found one another and rejoiced in that discovery.

And Paul thought how a bond encircled them, a ring. It was something that neither of them had any part in making, but rather, something that had been ordained from the beginning of time and was meant to be.

And suddenly, Paul thought about the ring of love. The name given to that very special ring of platinum and stone which his nona had given to him several years ago. The coincidence concerning its history and its future, in terms of the woman he now held in his arms, amazed him, a man who didn't believe in coincidence, and he squeezed Kristen closer to him, not wanting anything to ever twist that ring, that bond, which encircled them.

six

"I can't believe this is happening to me. . ." Kristen whispered into Paul's neck and he sighed, a deep, loving sound to her ears.

"Well," he paused for just a moment and lightly ran his hand over her cheek, "perhaps love at first sight runs in your family," he suggested, startling her.

"What?" She sat back and her eyes darted around his face in curious question.

"Sudden and forever lasting love has been know to happen to ancestors of yours before," he explained.

She looked at him in wonder. "Ancestors of mine?" She had never thought consciously in terms of her ancestors before. But now, as she thought about it, she knew that it was something that was very important to her, especially since she felt that sudden and unexpected love for this man.

He nodded and was again amazed that her father had never told her anything about her family history or that she had never thought to ask. "Weren't you ever the least bit curious about your ancestors?"

"I was but. . .I was told that I had no living relatives. . ." her voice trailed off and she lifted her eyebrows in mute explanation, "But I'm very curious about these ancestors of mine who loved. . .as we love," she finished shyly and rubbed her fingertips over the back of his hand. "Please tell me?"

He lifted his hand to the smoothness of her face and rejoiced when her eyes closed and she rubbed her face against his hand. Whimsically, he was reminded again of his little tabby cat back in Athens. That was her way of demonstrating her love for him. He couldn't help but think how Kristen had many other more wonderful ways of showing her love. But that kind of thinking was dangerous, especially while in her house alone. . .and at night. . .and in love. . . .

Abruptly Paul stood, startling Kristen's eyes open, and she watched questioningly as he strode over to the window which now showed only the shadow of night. "I think I saw a path leading down to the beach earlier?" he asked and she nodded her head in mute agreement, wondering what he had in mind.

Walking back to her, he took her hand and gently pulled her up from the sofa and over toward the deck. "Then let's take a walk on the beach and I'll tell you the story of the ring of love," he finished dramatically.

"The ring of love?" she questioned as they walked out onto the deck and he slid the door closed behind them.

"Ah. . .Kristen. Didn't you know that all good love stories have a name?"

"True," she agreed and laughed as they walked down the steps of the deck to reach the short but overgrown path which led to the beach. "Then tell me, Paul. . .what will our love story be called?"

She tilted her head femininely to the side, wondering what sort of a romantic title he would come up with.

"The Grecian Quest," he pronounced without hesitation while leading her over protruding roots and around tangled branches toward the pebbly beach.

"The Grecian Quest. . . ?" she echoed, dismayed by its lack of romance and in her disappointment she almost banged her head on a low branch.

"Careful," he admonished and pulled her around the branch and out onto the moonlit beach.

Turning to her, he watched as the long, silky strands of her hair were caught and played with by the strong wind. Lifted and twirled, her hair became a frame of motion around her face and he was glad that she hadn't cut it. He loved her hair and brought his fingers up to feel the strands as they danced in the wind.

But then, drawing his attention away from her hair to her eyes, he realized that she wasn't pleased about something. "Kristen? What is it?"

She shrugged her shoulders. "The Grecian Quest. . ." she repeated. "It's nice but. . .doesn't it sound more like the title for an adventure story than for a romance?"

Chuckling, he put his hands behind her neck and gently drew her close to him. "Ah. . .my sweet Kristen. But what could be more of an adventure than searching, finding, and learning all there is to know about our love?"

She sighed and smiled and let her head fall against his chest. The beating of his heart seemed to be one with the pounding of the surf. Together, they drummed out the rhythm of life, the adventure of life. The sea's steady rhythm brought with it the song of ages past and the man's heartbeat, the song of the present, and both told of people working and living and loving throughout time. As she stood and listened to the two together, the one with her right ear pressed against Paul's chest and the other with her left ear pressed by the sounds of the night, she knew that Paul was right. She was embarking on the greatest adventure of her life by traveling to Greece with him. And it would be an adventure meeting her blood relative, an adventure discovering if their sudden love was to be a long lasting love, and most of all, an adventure that might lead to their finding out about that Unknown, Something More. . . .

"Besides, other than giving this love of ours a chance to grow, aren't we going on an even greater quest together in Greece—in search for that Something More in life?" he asked, echoing her thoughts and Kristen was surprised, not by the question, but by the note of vulnerability she thought she heard creep into his voice. Leaving the beauty that came from listening to his beating heart, she stepped back from him and looked up into the warmth of his deep, dark eyes, eyes that were as dark and as deep as the summer night that surrounded them, and she realized, with something close to wonder, that like her, he too felt vulnerable over falling in love.

And suddenly, The Grecian Quest seemed like the perfect name for the love story that was becoming their very own. "Yes, Paul," she squeezed him closer to her and whispered assurance into his ear. "The greatest quest of our lives. . .our

Grecian Quest. . .and ours alone."

His hands hovered above her back for a second before finally having their way and pressing themselves against her slender shoulder blades. He wanted to kiss her, he wanted to love her, but even more, he wanted to give their love the chance to grow straight and sure without any bends or twists from yearnings being met prematurely, to chance ruining it. Besides, instinct told him that even if he pressed his desire, she was of morals that didn't allow certain bounds to be crossed. And for this he was glad, very, very glad.

Stepping away, Kristen took his hand and led him over to her favorite thinking spot, a sea log that had washed up on the beach long before Kristen had moved into her house. She pulled him down next to her. "Now tell me the story—The Ring of Love."

"Curious, aren't you?"

"Definitely!"

Smiling, he began. "Several years ago, when my Nona, your Aunt Aphrodite, was particularly concerned because I hadn't married, she presented me with a ring, a ring which has been in her family, your family that is, for over a century and a half."

Kristen hadn't remembered seeing a ring on Paul's hand but she felt along the knuckles of his hand anyway.

"No." He held up his hands for her to see that his fingers were void of rings. "It's not a man's ring. It's a woman's ring."

Her brows drew together in question. "Why would she give you a woman's ring?"

He smiled. "Its history will explain why."

"Sounds like it must have an interesting one."

"Believe me—it does." Paul took both of her hands in his. "Especially interesting since you and I. . .love. Another event in the long list of events that shows that Someone—perhaps God—is orchestrating the path of our lives—"

"Tell me," Kristen whispered.

"I've told you that your family comes from a very old shipping family." At her nod, he continued. "Well, let's see, it would have been your great-great-grandfather, whose name just happens to have been Paul, who started the tradition of the ring."

"My great-great-grandfather," she repeated wistfully. "And his name was Paul?" He nodded and she smiled. "I like the name." She raised her hand to his face and moved it along the strength of his jawline.

He turned his head and kissed her palm before guiding her hand back down to his other one. "The story gets better," his eyes narrowed, "but you'd better sit still if you want to hear it," he warned.

Paul couldn't know how happy it made her to know that he found her so attractive. Ted's last words to her had been that she was an, "ice queen, with a heart and a body made of ice." To know that Paul found her to be attractive and warm made her feel doubly so. But she wanted to hear the story so she primly folded her hands in her lap.

He nodded, satisfied, and continued. "During the golden days of Galaxidi, which was one of the major shipping ports of Greece during the last century, your ancestor, who was a wealthy shipowner, survived a very dangerous trip around the Cape of Good Hope. By all accounts, he should have died. He had been injured, was taken sick, and the weather was supposed to have been fierce. But against all odds he survived the trip."

"Now that's an adventure!" Kristen interjected.

Paul smiled and continued, "Well, he was certain that he'd survived because of the prayers of his much loved wife back in far-off Greece, whose name just happened to have been . . .Christina."

"Christina! My grandmother's name! My name. . ." she whispered in awe.

"Your name is a chain through the history of your family, Kristen. Remember how I told you that it's a tradition to name children after their grandparents. . .well, through your grandmother, you were named for the Christina of our story."

Kristen shook her head in wonder. "It's amazing. . ."

He nodded his head in agreement and taking her hand in his and twining his fingers through hers, continued, "Even though their marriage had been arranged, as all marriages were in those days, they fell instantly in love with one another within moments of meeting." He paused and kissed her forehead.

Kristen nuzzled up against his shoulder. "Sudden love. . ." she whispered.

"And forever-lasting love," Paul reminded her of the second part, draping his arm around her shoulder to gather her closer to him.

"Forever-lasting. . ." Kristen repeated, her voice sounding like liquid crystal to Paul's ears. "Well, so far we have the sudden love, and our names in common with the hero and heroine of the ring of love. . .the 'forever-lasting' must follow." She looked up at him and he didn't think that he had ever seen a more beautiful pair of eyes. *Emeralds, and that includes the unusual emerald in the ring of love, would be lucky if they looked half as beautiful,* he thought, and gently brushed his lips across the smoothness of her lids. She raised her lips to meet his but he turned away with a groan.

"Kristen. . .do you want to hear the story or not?"

She smiled and turning her face toward the singing sea, settled back against his side, determined not to interrupt again. But she reveled in knowing that he found her attractive.

"Good," he cleared his throat and continued. "Well, the truth was, somehow Christina sensed that something was wrong with her beloved husband. And even when she was heavy with her surprise to him—their son—she was to be found, day and night, in the chapel of their home praying for his safe return. Paul survived that voyage and with practically all the money he earned from it he bought a ring, a most unusual ring. . ."

"The ring of love. . ." Kristen whispered the words into the wind, which danced around their heads before being carried off into the windy night.

"That's right," Paul agreed. "And from the day Paul came home and put the ring on Christina's finger she wore it and your great-great-grandfather Paul always returned to his Christina from all his journeys to finally end his days a very old man at his wife's side, something very unusual back in those days of sailing ships and pirates. People always said that it was her love and her prayers for him that always brought him back to her when other women's husbands didn't survive."

"Oh, how lovely. . ." Kristen said dreamily.

"The ring has come to symbolize their love and faith."

"But," she swiveled her head to look up at him, "I still don't understand why my aunt gave you a woman's ring?"

"There is more about the ring. It is to be worn only by married or engaged women of the Vasilias family and since I was a member of the family by being your Aunt Aphrodite's godson, and since she had no idea where you were, she gave it to me to put on the finger of my bride."

Kristen sat up straight. To fall in love in one afternoon was one thing but to talk about marriage all in the same afternoon was something entirely different, especially after the disaster of her marriage to Ted.

"Paul. . ." she began, but he cut her off with a chuckle that instantly relieved her.

"Don't worry, Kristen. . .I'm not proposing. . ."

She glanced over at him and at his warm smile, smiled self-consciously back at him. "It's just that. . .we have so much ahead of us. . .my aunt. . .our search. . ."

"I agree."

"You do? Honestly?"

"I do. Even though I know that I'm no longer falling in love with you. . ."

She knew from his velvety-sounding voice with its magical accent that something wonderful was coming and with the patience of one hearing a fairy tale unfold, knowing that a happy ending was in store, she waited to hear him speak.

"Because you see. . ." he rubbed her face with his hand, "I've already fallen. . .I'm there. . .I love you."

"Oh, Paul. . ." she whispered as their foreheads touched. "I love you too." And then their lips touched, and then their souls, as they became one with the elements of the Pacific night.

"Darling Kristen," Paul whispered her name after a tiny moment.

"As the only direct descendant of Paul and Christina, the ring of love is yours to wear upon your engagement—" he rubbed the fourth finger on her left hand, "but I hope—that the ring of love in your life—will include me—"

"Oh, Paul. . .I feel sure that it will. . .someday. . .it's just that. . .before I make any plans. . ."

"I know—" he cut her off. "And I agree." And before her amazed eyes he repeated the verse they had discussed earlier, " 'You have made known to me the path of life. . .' "

Kristen nodded her head. "You really do understand."

"I think—somehow—that our quest is very important—to our love." He spoke haltingly but with such emotion that Kristen felt tears sting her eyes.

"Oh, Paul. . ." she gently went to rest her head against his chest, but a noise coming from the sea that was different from the pounding of the waves meeting land, made her stop.

Both turned their heads toward the sound.

"Did you hear something?"

She nodded her head, "I thought I heard a cry—"

"Help. . .someone. . .help. . ." The faint cry came to them again above the pounding of the surf and both Kristen and Paul were on their feet and running toward the dark, foaming sea from where it came.

"Somebody's out there!" Paul, now a couple of strides ahead of Kristen, yelled into the wind.

"Help me!" The plea sounded again just as Paul flung off his shoes and jacket and dashed into the crashing waves to swim toward the unknown person.

Kristen kicked off her pumps and ran to where the waves beat against her waist but there she stopped, knowing that she would do more harm than good if she attempted to swim the turbulent sea. Unlike Paul, she was not a very good swimmer. She could barely keep herself afloat in calm seas, much less save someone else and in such turbulent seas. Watching Paul swim, now on top of the waves, now lost on the other side, she marveled at how on this night, the first where there had ever been a cry of need from the ocean below her home,

Paul was there to help her. She didn't know what she would have done if she had been alone.

As it was, the waves pushed and pulled against her, threatening to lift her feet out from under her. Her flowered skirt billowed out in the waves, like a lifesaver. Kristen wished that it was one.

From the pale gibbous moon that was only now showing its face above Mount Tamalpais, Kristen watched as Paul closed the distance between himself and the man, and she could almost feel Paul's relief as he grabbed the driftwood which the man was clinging to and propelled him toward shore.

She watched and prayed, as all people seem to pray when they're frightened, whether they know God or not, and willed Paul to come to shore. Paul pushed through the water with his powerful muscles, man against the sea, now eight, now five, now three yards away to finally reach Kristen.

With his last ounce of strength Paul pushed the man, still clinging to the log, toward Kristen. "Get him to shore!" he yelled.

Kristen grabbed ahold of the driftwood and with all her might pulled the man the final yards to shore. Twice she fell down as the combination of the man's weight, the pounding waves, and the strong Pacific undertow all fought against her efforts. And when the driftwood slammed against her knees she had a moment of horror when she thought she was going to lose her battle, but Paul was now by her side and together they fought the sea to get the man ashore.

"Dear God, help us," Kristen petitioned out loud and laughed giddily as a huge wave immediately surged against the driftwood and flung her, the man, and Paul onto the shore.

The three lay panting for a few minutes before Kristen raised herself to her knees and with all her remaining strength, pulled the man away from the waves and up onto the dry beach.

"Thank God. . ." the man whispered as the dry sand touched his exhausted body and only then did he release his grip on the driftwood that had probably saved his life. "Thank God . . ." he looked up at Kristen, his eyes red and puffy, but much to Kristen's joy they were focused and alert. "After coming so far. . .I didn't have the energy to come ashore. . .I saw a light . . .and I prayed. . ." he coughed and Kristen helped him to discharge whatever of the sea he had swallowed and with a look that said he thought he was looking at an angel, he continued, "I prayed that you were on the shore. . .thank you. . ." he shut his eyes and Kristen gently laid him back down on the sand. He was exhausted and had already fallen asleep.

She looked over at Paul. Stumbling over to the man's side, on legs that felt like jelly, Paul reached for the unconscious man's pulse and was glad to feel it strong against his numb fingertips and quickly running his hands over the man's body, confirmed that there were no broken bones.

He looked over at Kristen, and reached for her. "We make a good team."

She squeezed his hand and smiled and when he shook his head like a dog, the thought amazingly came to her that now that his hair had been touched by the sea, he was identical to the *Youth of Antikythera.*

She laughed, a light, free laugh of happiness, of relief, of joy that sailed off into the night like a seagull at dawn.

Paul smiled with her and looked down at the man. "I think he's going to be fine."

Nodding, happiness enabling her to stand on her wobbly feet, she said, "You stay with him while I call 9-1-1 and bring some blankets and hot soup."

"Soup. . ." the man mumbled, opening his eyes a bit. "Sounds wonderful. . .so glad God let our paths meet. . ." he whispered before drifting off into an exhausted sleep once again.

For just a second, Paul's eyes met Kristen's. They were both thinking the same thing. "The path of life. . ." and how glad they were that they had walked the path down to the beach that night. . .for so many reasons.

"I love you," Paul mouthed the words and before Kristen dashed off to her house, she mouthed the words back to him.

And she had never meant anything more in her life.

seven

"I can't remember when I've ever been so sore, Uncle George," Kristen said the next evening to the dignified man who sat on the sofa next to her in her living room. "But it's a good kind of sore," she amended and smiling, rubbed her stiff arms. Knowing that she had helped to save a man's life was a heady feeling.

"I'm proud of you, Kristy." George's voice was as dignified as his appearance. With a thick head of white, not gray, hair, and a tall, slender physique which men twenty years his junior could normally only hope to have, Kristen's Uncle George was a man the world took seriously. But right now his eyes twinkled as they always did for his best friend's daughter. That he loved Kristen as a beloved uncle might was readily obvious. "And your parents would be, too."

She looked down. "I wish they had been able to swim to shore. . .when their boat sank. . ."

George reached over and patted Kristen's hand. She looked up at him and the sadness she saw there reminded her that he missed them as much as she did. And she didn't want him to be sad. Taking a deep breath that was meant to brighten the mood, she said, "Well, I'm just glad Paul was here. I never could have fought those waves and brought that man to safety alone."

When George cleared his throat and sat forward on the sofa Kristen knew that she had said the wrong thing. He had made himself clear on the phone the previous night that he didn't like the idea of her going to visit her Aunt Aphrodite and especially with a man who was a stranger. "Kristy, what do you know about this man?"

Kristen smiled, a secret smile which George saw and which did nothing to relieve his apprehensions. His frown lines deepened across his brow. That George was worried about Kristen traveling to Greece was obvious to her, so how could she worry him further by telling him that what she knew about Paul Andrakos was that she loved him, she needed him, she wanted to be with him always.

"What work does he do?" George persisted, cutting into Kristen's thoughts.

It amazed Kristen to consider that she really didn't know what job Paul actually did. His worth to her didn't come from his profession. It came from the man himself, that essence which was Paul Andrakos. But she knew that like her parents, her Uncle George wouldn't understand that, so somewhat on the defensive side she answered, "Paul's a business associate of my aunt's. You do know what my aunt does?"

"Of course." He answered and Kristen lifted an elegant eyebrow at the defensive quality in his tone. It was an unusual timbre to hear in George.

"What else do you know? Did you know that my parents were planning a trip to Greece?" She pressed her advantage, both amazed and relieved to have shifted the direction of the subject. Uncle George was a lawyer who rarely lost the upper hand.

"Yes. I knew that there was some sort of reconciliation and that they were planning to visit your aunt," he admitted in his best lawyer's voice.

Kristen raised her hands in exasperation. "It seems like everyone knows things about my family and its history—everyone except for me that is!"

George ignored her outburst and remained calm and serious. "Kristen," he caught her attention at his use of her full name and effectively cut off her exasperated anger. He rarely called her anything but "Kristy" and "Darling." For him to use her full name meant that the subject was of great importance to him. The last time he'd used it was to tell her that her parents had perished in a boating accident. "Don't go to Greece."

She took a deep breath and immediately softened toward

him. The fact that her parents hadn't told her anything about her family wasn't his fault after all. He had always been a great friend to her, a man who had become a beloved uncle to her out of love for her and her parents, fulfilling a great need in her life. "Uncle George," she reached over for his hand. "But why? Why don't you want me to go?"

"Kristy—" he paused and rubbed her smooth hand between both of his. He seemed to be weighing his words. "I don't think your father would want you to go."

Kristen shook her head. "I don't agree with you, Uncle George. I think that he would want me to go. . .as if I'm going in his place. And according to Paul, my aunt really wants to meet me."

"Kristy—" he seemed to be choosing his words carefully, "sometimes friends are better than relatives. You haven't been around relatives so you've romanticized everything to do with them."

And with these words Kristen thought she understood what was bothering the older man. "Uncle George. . .are you afraid that my aunt might take your place in my affections? Because if you are. . ."

"No, Kristy. . .of course not," he denied hotly.

"No one could take your place in my life," she finished stubbornly. "You've been the greatest uncle a girl could ever wish for."

With a sigh, he pursed his lips together and sat back. "Kristy—I am not afraid of anyone taking my 'place.' However, I am concerned that you will be hurt," he paused and reaching out for her hand, squeezed it. "Darling girl—you have been hurt too much during the last couple of years."

She pulled her hand away and snapped, "And I have been a recluse because of it." Jumping up from the sofa, Kristen strode over to the window and stood looking out at the path which led to the beach.

She remembered all the times during the last year that she had walked that path alone. And then she remembered the previous night and how she had walked that same path with

Paul and how they had talked about a path that might lead them to a future together and then, how their path had met another person's path which meant saving that man's life. *Not a bad way to start a life together,* Kristen thought, and turning back to Uncle George, she thought how she had done more living the previous day than she had done during the entire previous year and a half.

"I'm going to Greece, Uncle George," she said with finality. "I believe it's what I'm meant to do."

Like a father who had tried to talk sense into his child but finally had to admit to the futility of it, George sighed and standing, walked over to Kristen. Holding her shoulders lightly between his hands, he smiled down at her, a smile that told of all the love he felt for his best friend's daughter. "Then God bless, my darling girl—" he grimaced, "I just wish that I didn't have to be in China during the next few months and in such a remote location."

"But why?"

"So that you could call me if you needed anything."

Kristen wrapped her arms around his neck and hugged him as she had hugged him ever since she was a little girl. "Uncle George! Don't worry, I won't need anything," she whispered and stepped away. "I'm a big girl now—remember?"

The doorbell rang and Kristen looked happily toward the door. "That must be Paul." She stood on her tiptoes and lightly kissed her uncle's cheek before hurrying toward the door. "You're going to like him," she threw back over her shoulder before reaching for the doorknob.

She opened the door and laughed delightedly as Paul presented her with a beautiful bouquet of fragrant roses, roses of every shade.

"Flowers again!" she laughed and nuzzled her nose among their silky folds. "But we're leaving tomorrow night. What will I do with them?"

"You will enjoy them until then and when we get to Athens, there will be a white bouquet for you," he said and kissed her in the European fashion of a quick peck on both cheeks. He wanted to do much more, but he could see the man whom he knew must be her Uncle George from the corner of his eye.

"White roses?"

"Don't tell me that you've never heard of the white roses of Athens? There's even a song about them."

She laughed again. "Then you will have to sing it to me."

"Ah. . .no. Singing is not one of my talents. We'll leave the singing of that song to Nana Mouscouri."

"Nana who?"

"A Greek singer who sings like a nightingale," Paul explained as Kristen led him over to where George was standing by the window watching their exchange with interest and in spite of their restraint, with understanding. It would take a very obtuse person not to notice that there was more to Kristen and Paul's relationship than just friendship. And Kristen's Uncle George was not obtuse about anything.

"Uncle George," she introduced the older man to the younger, "I'd like for you to meet Paul Andrakos." She turned to Paul. "Paul, this is George Lee, whom I fondly refer to as my 'Uncle' George."

The two men shook hands and in the moment that it took to do so, they sized one another up as men all over the world do upon meeting. Both of them, in spite of their desires not to, liked what they saw in the other. This assessment was obvious to Kristen and made her very happy.

George's eyes narrowed. "Andrakos?" he questioned. "The Mr. Andrakos who just completed the amazing merging of Star with Achilles shipping lines?"

Paul smiled. He was surprised by the inquiry. "Yes, the same," he admitted. "But it's very recent. I'm surprised that you've heard about it?"

"I'm a corporate lawyer." George explained. "I just read about the merging in yesterday's International Corporate News and I've always kind of kept an eye on the Achilles Line," George explained.

"Achilles line?" Kristen questioned.

"One of your aunt's—and my—shipping interests," Paul

explained to her but continued to look at George. "You know about Kristen's family?" he questioned.

George shrugged his shoulders. "Nick King, Kristen's father, told me a few things," he said carefully, *too carefully,* Paul thought, and he wondered how much the older man actually knew. For some reason, Paul was quite certain that he knew a lot more about past events than he let on. Paul wouldn't forget this. Certain things were good to remember. This item was one of them.

"Why don't we all sit down?" Kristen suggested and the two men politely sat on opposite sofas. Kristen sat on the same sofa as Paul, which made him very happy. He wanted to reach across the small space and take ahold of her hand but with George Lee watching, he didn't. She smiled over at him and he could tell that she was thinking the same thing.

"Mr. Andrakos—" George began, "I have to admit that I'm not too pleased over Kristen traveling to Greece with you."

"Uncle George!" Kristen turned to him, totally surprised that he would say such a thing. It was so out of character for him to be so forward.

But he ignored her and continued, looking piercingly only at Paul. "I don't want to see her hurt." That quality which made most people tremble when George Lee spoke was in evidence. But looking over at Paul, Kristen wasn't surprised to see that Paul neither trembled nor wavered but rather was a match for her uncle. "Believe me, sir—neither do I." Paul answered politely.

"She has been hurt too much in the past—" George persisted.

"I will do everything in my power to make sure she is not hurt in the future," Paul declared.

But Kristen had had enough of them talking as though she wasn't there. "Would you two stop. . .you're acting as though I'm a child."

Her uncle ignored her. He wanted some answers from Paul and he wanted them now. "But does her aunt really want to see her or just nurse her bad conscience?"

Paul smiled over at Kristen to assure her that he wasn't trying to talk over her and then answered George. "A lot of the first and probably a little bit of the second," Paul replied truthfully. "Who, when they reach the age of Aphrodite, doesn't want to assuage their conscience?"

Kristen watched her uncle. He liked that response and smiled. "Kristen said she'd been sick?"

Paul nodded. "Heart problems."

"Does she know that Kristen is coming?"

At that Paul turned to Kristen. "I talked to your aunt earlier today." In spite of the watchful eyes of the older man Paul took her hand in his. "She is thrilled to hear that you are coming. She'll be calling you," the phone rang out shrilly and Paul motioned toward it and smiled, "this evening."

Kristen glanced over at Uncle George. There was no condemnation in him. Since he couldn't change her mind he was now supporting her decision. She smiled her thanks.

As she walked over to the phone, she couldn't quite believe that this might be the phone call she had been waiting so expectantly for all those months. All of a sudden she felt very nervous and very shy. She placed her hand on the receiver and glanced over at Paul.

"She's a very nice lady," he assured her.

She nodded and picked up the phone. "Hello?"

There was a slight pause as the transatlantic connection was made and then Kristen heard her aunt's voice for the very first time in her life. "Hello. Is this Christina King?" The use of the name "Christina" threw Kristen for a moment, not because she was offended but rather because she liked the way it sounded. She was a descendent of the Christina in the ring of love and Kristen liked this link with her ancestry, this link through time.

She made a quick decision not to correct the older woman. "Yes, this is. Are you my Aunt Aphrodite?"

"Oh my dear. . .I am. But I have waited too many years to hear that title." It was a cultured voice, a rounded voice, a voice of authority which was slightly accented by a multitude of languages.

"Aunt Aphrodite. . .I'm so glad you contacted me. . .I didn't know what to think when I didn't hear from you. . ."

"Please forgive me," the older woman asked through the lines, and modern technology made it seem as though she was in the next room, not halfway around the world. "But Paul explained the circumstances?"

"Yes. . .don't worry. . .I understand. Just stay well."

"I'm trying, my dear, I'm trying. . .but Christina, your coming with Paul means everything to me. I would have come to you if I had been able to do so. Unfortunately, my mind is willing but my body is not. . ."

"Well, both my mind and body are willing so I will see you in just a couple of days, Aunt."

"In just a couple of days. . ." her aunt whispered, "after a lifetime."

When they hung up, Kristen looked at the two men who were looking at her so expectantly and smiled, a smile which her Uncle George was familiar with but hadn't seen in a couple of years and a smile which made Paul feel as if the sun had come out after months of dark, dreary winter skies.

"I know that I've made the correct decision in going!" she exclaimed. "I can't wait to see my aunt!"

George smiled and stood to leave. "I'm glad."

Kristen walked over to him and hugged him. "You don't have to worry, Uncle George. . .that lady," she motioned with her head toward the phone, "loves me. She really wants to see me."

"I'm not worried, Kristy." He looked over at Paul. "I have Mr. Andrakos's word that you will not be hurt." He smiled at Paul. "And from all the years of following Achilles Industries, I know that Mr. Andrakos's word is good."

Paul stood and extended his hand. "Thank you, sir. Thank you for your trust."

That the two men trusted one another filled Kristen with gladness and she knew that the picture of them shaking hands would stay with her forever. That thought reminded her about actual pictures which she wanted to show her uncle.

"Oh! Uncle George. . .before you leave. . ." she walked over to an end table and opening it, reached for the four photographs which she had left lying conveniently on top. "When I went through my parents' papers. . .I found these photographs." She extended the pictures to him but frowned slightly at her uncle's intake of breath. She hadn't even considered that seeing the photos might upset him. "I'm sorry. . .I should have warned you," she offered.

He waved her apology aside. "No. . .it's just that," he glanced through the pictures, "these were taken," he paused and breathed out, "a lifetime ago."

"At least two lifetimes ago," Kristen whispered and pointed to her parents. "I recognize my father and my mother and you. . .but who was this man?" She pointed to a man with laughing green eyes and dark wavy hair who had his arm draped casually around Kristen's mother in three photos but was alone with her in the fourth.

"That," George paused as if remembering the man fondly, "was Raphael. He was from Spain and one of the nicest, most fun loving persons anyone could ever hope to meet."

"Was?" Kristen questioned.

George nodded sadly. "Unfortunately he was also one of the world's most daring men. He was a Rally racer. These pictures were taken in Monte Carlo where he was racing. He died the next day."

"Oh, how sad." Kristen pointed to the last picture. It was the one of just Kristen's mother, Jane, and Raphael looking at one another with a look that reminded Kristen of how she probably looked at Paul. She frowned. They definitely looked like they were in love but not wanting to upset her Uncle George, she said, "They look like they were very good friends."

"Even more than friends," Paul spoke Kristen's thought and she was glad for the chance to ask her uncle. That was what had bothered her since she had first found the photos.

"Were they, Uncle George?"

"No. No. Just friends."

Paul looked at the older man quizzically. He seemed to answer too quickly, as if he had something to hide.

"You know that your mother only had eyes for your father," George was quick to qualify.

Kristen nodded. "That's for sure." She handed the pictures to George, "Would you like to keep them. . .since you were there. . ."

George took them and giving the top one another glance said, "We were all the best of friends. I miss them all and I would very much like to keep these photos. A remembrance of a very lovely day." He put them in his suit pocket. "Thank you, my darling girl."

George and Paul nodded at one another before Kristen walked with her uncle to the door.

"Thanks for coming. . ."

George reached out his hand and rubbed her arm. "Couldn't let Jane and Nick's little girl's birthday pass without seeing her." He smiled and his lips seemed to move to control the emotion he was feeling. "Don't ever forget. . .they loved you more than anything. . .or anyone. . .in the world."

Kristen nodded. "I know. . .I won't forget." They kissed and then the older man was gone into the night.

Turning back to Paul, Kristen smiled. "That's my Uncle George," she said simply.

"A nice man." He walked toward her. "I think I had better be going too."

"So soon?" The disappointment she felt was in her deep voice.

"We have a plane to catch tomorrow," he reminded her. "Don't you have some packing to do?"

Kristen shrugged. "I guess. . ." She walked up to him and boldly put her hands around his neck. "But I still don't want you to leave."

Paul chuckled. "I think it's a good thing that you will be staying with your aunt in Athens."

"Why?"

He nuzzled his nose against her neck and sighing, gently

stood away from her. "Because I don't think it's a good idea for us to be alone in an empty house, feeling the way we do."

"Paul—I've never—nor would I ever—" she stopped and looking at him realized that with him, she might. She had never felt such an attraction for a man before; in fact until Paul, she'd had no idea that someone could feel such desires. She stepped back from him. "I see what you mean," she whispered.

He smiled, a smile of yearning, a smile of want, but more than anything, a smile of love.

"I'll pick you up tomorrow at around three."

"You don't have to. I'll call a cab."

"Nonsense. I'll leave my rental car at the airport anyway." His eyes deepened along with his voice. "And besides—I want to start our quest together from your house."

"Me too." Her voice was deep and husky and if the phone hadn't chosen that moment to ring, Paul wasn't sure that he would have been able to prevent himself from going to her, empty house or not.

"I'll just be a moment," Kristen turned and reached for the phone. It was the man that she and Paul had pulled out from the ocean the previous night.

Paul looked over in interest when he understood who it was and asked, "Is he okay?"

Kristen nodded yes to Paul and continued to talk into the phone to the man. "You're what?" she asked and it was obvious to Paul that she was surprised by something. "That's amazing. I'm going to be traveling to Athens tomorrow and Paul—the man who was with me—is from Athens." Paul looked at her in question. Her eyes were wide in wonder as she finished talking to the man.

"Well, be careful of wind surfing in Pacific waves, Dean, and I'm looking forward to seeing you next week."

"Next week?" Paul questioned her while taking the phone.

Kristen nodded and looked at Paul deeply, meaningfully. "You're not going to believe this—he's a pastor at a church in—in Athens."

"In Athens?" he repeated. She was right. He didn't believe it.

She nodded and motioned to the phone. Paul talked animatedly for a few moments, gave the man his address and phone number in Athens, and after hanging up, stood looking out at the ocean which was as calm today as it had been treacherous the day before.

Kristen walked up behind him. "Paul?"

He shook his head "It's amazing. He again said something about being glad that our paths—met with his last night—"

"Paths. . ." Kristen whispered and looked out at the calm, somnolent sea. "If it hadn't been windy yesterday—"

"—he wouldn't have needed our help."

"Is he Greek?"

Paul tilted his head upward. "No. He's American. An American Pastor serving at an American, interdenominational church in Athens. I wonder if it's the one Lottie wrote about?"

Paul walked over to the coffee table and picked up the Bible Lottie had sent to Kristen the previous day. "Kristen—I found a Bible in my hotel room—and read some of it last night—the part about St. Paul in Athens. Kristen—do you know what he said?"

Kristen shook her head, wonder filled her eyes. "Tell me."

"'Men of Athens!' Men of Athens—" Paul repeated. "Kristen, I'm one of those 'Men of Athens'!"

"It's like he's talking directly to you—"

Paul nodded. "And something else. He said something about telling them about the God they worship as something unknown. . .something unknown. . ."

With an excitement Paul hadn't felt since he was a very little boy, he continued, "Kristen, when we get to Athens, I want us to visit the Biblical sites and find out where they are written about in the Bible."

Kristen nodded. "Our search."

"Our quest."

"Together. . ." Kristen whispered and stepped into Paul's outstretched arms.

"The pastor will call me when he returns to Athens in a few days," he held her tightly against him for a moment and then stepping away, placed the Bible back on the table next to the little statue of the *Youth of Antikythera* and continued on toward the door. "Good night, my love. . .don't forget to pack your Bible," he said as he placed his hand on the doorknob.

"Paul!" Kristen ran up to him, surprised that he was really intent on leaving. "You really don't have to go so soon."

He turned to her and with a look that showed just what it was costing him to be near her, answered back, his accent making his words sound like a loving caress, a caress that touched her soul.

"Ah. . .my love. . .but I do."

eight

"I don't think I've ever seen such a pretty approach to an airport," Kristen exclaimed nearly two days later as the jet she and Paul were traveling on made its descent into Hellenicon International Airport in Athens.

"Those islands look like the Titans." She glanced over at Paul, "The supposed parents to the Olympian gods," she explained, "dropped bits of earth on their way to making the mountains of Greece."

Paul chuckled and then frowned in concentration. "Except—if I remember correctly—the ancient Greeks never attributed the creation of the world to their gods. Rather, the gods were created by the universe."

Kristen answered thoughtfully. "Maybe that's one of the reasons Greece became a Biblical land."

"What do you mean?"

"Well. . .the Greeks already accepted that their gods were created by the universe. They were thinkers. Maybe they were ready to accept that the universe could not just come into being anymore than," she paused searching around for a good example, "one of their temples could just appear."

Paul tipped his head in appreciation of her analogy. "I see what you mean."

She continued her thought. "Maybe—they were ready to hear about Someone—a God—who claimed to have made the universe."

Paul took her hand in his and gently squeezed it. "Just like—we're ready to hear about that God too."

Kristen nodded and whispered, "So much has changed from one week ago." The sound of the jet engines using their might to slow the plane almost drowned out her words.

"But you're glad?" Paul asked. He wanted assurance.

Kristen moved her head up and down, slowly, thoughtfully. "So glad. . .because of you. . .my aunt. . .our search. . ." she paused and repeated again, "and you. . ." and then met him in a kiss, just a simple kiss but a kiss that held love, caring, and hope for a future together.

With their foreheads touching, Paul chuckled wryly. "Well, if I know your aunt, she's probably looking expectantly at the clock every few moments wondering if our plane has landed."

Kristen sat back. That surprised her. "Really? I pictured her as being totally cool and very patient."

Paul shook his head and his eyes widened at thinking about the older woman. "Not Aphrodite. Oh, she can be cool. In the business world no one ever knows what she's thinking," he amended. "But in her personal life, she's a mother hen who worries and clucks and drives James and me crazy."

"James?"

"Her best friend. An English lord, and nearly her own age. James is probably the only person in this world who Aphrodite listens to."

Kristen was very surprised by this character sketch of her aunt and it showed in her face.

"I've shocked you?" Paul inquired with a raised brow.

Kristen nodded. "I just pictured her. . .differently." She paused for a moment and then with a seriousness in her tone asked, "Paul. . .?"

He looked at her in question, waiting.

"I've been thinking. . ." she wasn't sure how Paul would take her next words so she spoke carefully, gently, and touched her fingers lightly to his arm. "Maybe we shouldn't let my aunt know how we feel. . .about one another. . .just yet. . ."

"But why?" Paul's surprise over the suggestion showed in the sudden tilting of his head.

"I think. . .I think it might be too much for her. . ." Kristen boldly continued, hoping that Paul would understand, "especially after you telling me how she frets about people about whom she cares."

Paul seemed to consider her words. "I don't know, Kristen—

Nona knows me too well—I think she'll catch on pretty quickly."

"Well. . .let's try. . .at least for a couple of days not to let her know. I think it's important. . .to my relationship with her."

Paul's eyes scanned her face. He was amazed by Kristen's astuteness. Knowing Aphrodite as he did, he should have been the one to understand that detecting a relationship between Kristen and himself, immediately upon arrival, might be too much for the older lady. She and Kristen needed the time to forge a bond without any outside interferences. And Paul knew that seeing him in a serious relationship with any woman would be enough to excite the older woman. How much more with her own niece? He had no fear that his nona would mind him being interested in her niece, but he knew that Kristen was right in suggesting that they not hit her over the head with the knowledge.

"I love you," he finally whispered.

Kristen wrapped her arms around his neck and whispered into his ear, "Oh, Paul. . .I love you too." She raised her face to his.

"And you do understand?" She wanted to make sure that there was no misunderstanding.

He raised his brows self-deprecatingly. "I should have been the one to suggest it." He took her hand in his. "I promise . . .I'll try very hard to hide my feelings." He took a deep breath. "But, it won't be easy," he was quick to interject.

"I know. For me either."

"I do have a great deal of business to attend to these first few days. I'll use that as an excuse not to be around too much."

"Oh, Paul. . .I'll miss you."

"Hey! Only for a few days—Aphrodite will have to be told after that."

Kristen nodded. "Thank you, Paul."

"No. Thank you, Kristen." He tapped her on the tip of her nose. "I want both of the women in my life, you and my nona, to be happy."

"We've had a few days to get used to our love. Let's give Aphrodite a few as well."

The plane tilted to the left and Paul's glance was pulled to the sea view out the window over Kristen's shoulder. "Look at that." He nodded out the little window. "I've flown all over the world but I've never seen bluer bodies of water than those found around Greece."

She followed his eyes to look down at the Saronic Gulf. It was the bluest sea she had ever seen, as blue as little children show seas to be when they color them with their crayons. "Such a deep shade. Almost cobalt," she agreed before wistfully adding, "my father's eyes were like that."

Paul looked at her in surprise. "Really?"

Kristen motioned down to the sea, which was getting closer and closer as the jet was about to land. "As blue as that water."

"Aphrodite's eyes are like that too," Paul commented.

Kristen shook her head in wonder. That there might be a resemblance between her aunt and her father wasn't even something she had previously considered. The thought thrilled her, especially since Kristen didn't resemble her father at all.

"I can't wait to meet her," she whispered and squeezed Paul's hand as the plane's landing gear made contact with the asphalt at Athens international airport. After taxiing down the runway, the huge metal bird turned and followed the path to the terminal.

Kristen was on the same soil as her aunt now. She glanced over at Paul. She was in the "Man from Greece's" land. And she was glad with her choice to be there to discover her path in life.

❧

Kristen's first ride through Athens was a trip she knew that she would never forget. To say that the city was vibrant and alive would be only a half truth. It was more than that. It was dusty and hot, noisy and fast, and yet at the same moment it was clean and cool, serene and slow. Mountains encircled the city on the east, north, and west with the Saronic Gulf being the boundary on the south, making the plain of Athens a foundation for low buildings of concrete and marble.

People grasping plastic bags, and cars with honking horns seemed to be everywhere. And just when Kristen didn't think she could stand seeing any more nondescript, smog-dirtied, flat buildings, a twist in the road revealed the graceful columns of a temple from the elegant past as it rose, even with the road in front of her. She let out a gasp of pleasure.

"What is that?"

"The Temple of the Olympian Zeus."

"It's beautiful."

"It is." Paul made a turn and pointed up and out the side window. "But it's nothing compared to that."

Kristen gasped again but this time it was a gasp of knowledge.

She had no doubt that what her eyes rested on was the Acropolis of Athens.

"Oh, Paul."

She didn't take her eyes off the flat mountaintop. Covered with some of the world's most beautiful architectural structures, including that most graceful and elegant of buildings, the Parthenon, it was a sight that held Kristen spellbound.

"Please. . .may we stop for a moment?"

He chuckled and pulled the car off to the side of the road next to the ancient Theater of Dionysus. The sidewalk was filled with tourists from the world over—Asians, Europeans, Africans, Americans—all come to see the world renowned Acropolis, the High City, the citadel, that sat like a jewel above the modern city of Athens. But the commotion of people didn't bother Kristen in the least. She scrambled out of the car and stood, surrounded by the throng of holiday seeking people, hugging her arms around her.

Paul touched her. She had goosebumps on her arms.

"In this heat, you can't be cold."

Kristen shook her head but still didn't remove her eyes from the Acropolis. The Parthenon, that most beautiful of classical buildings, that was built during the golden age of Pericles, sat timeless and elegant against the blue of the Grecian sky.

"I'm. . .amazed. . .it's more beautiful than I ever dreamed. I could stand and look at it all day long," she murmured in awe.

Paul drew her close to him. "And I could do the same with you," he whispered. "But," he reached for the door handle of the car, his arm still around her shoulder, "I think that we had better go. Your aunt will be waiting for you and not very patiently."

Kristen smiled her agreement, and turned away from the Acropolis and stepped into the car. She enjoyed sitting back and watching the modern city of Athens as it slid past her window. The center of Athens was a busy place with people going about their business much as they do in New York and London, Cape Town and Hong Kong.

Colorful kiosks selling anything from razor blades to newspapers were to be seen at practically every corner and motorbikes scurrying around like bugs on wheels scuttled between and around the cars, none holding a lane, and all terrifying Kristen.

After a few more minutes of congested driving conditions, Paul stopped at an overpass to turn off the main boulevard, and pointed ahead, "Your aunt's neighborhood is just over there."

"So soon?" Kristen was surprised, especially when she saw how different the suburb was from the city they had passed through. Quiet streets that were lined with trees and plants of a multitude of varieties surrounded her. Graceful and feminine eucalyptus trees swayed in the soft wind, hardy pines added their deep green color to the quiet streets, while oleander bushes, the size of small trees, scented the air with their pink and white flowers.

Kristen looked at Paul in amazement. "It's so peaceful here. I can't believe we're so close to the city."

"Old Psychikon, the name of this area, is the first garden suburb outside of the city, and a world all its own. Nona can't understand why I ever left it."

"You used to live here too?"

He nodded. "Like your father, I grew up here."

"This is where my father grew up. . ." Kristen mused and looking at the quiet streets, she tried to imagine him as a young man walking or riding his bike along these actual streets. But try as she may she couldn't. She didn't know enough about her father's youth to even begin to picture him as a young man and for all its beauty, it was too different from American neighborhoods for her to even try. There were sidewalks, but they were often uneven or overgrown with bushes or cut in the middle by trees. In many cases cars had parked up on the sidewalks as the roads were too narrow to allow them to remain parked at the side of the road.

Most of the houses had walls around them and those that didn't had bushes or trees hiding them from passersby. After a moment Paul turned into one of the sidewalks and paused in front of a large door. He pressed a button on the dashboard and the door started to slide back from the left.

"Welcome to your ancestral home, Kristen."

Like a curtain on a stage, the door slowly opened to reveal a large neoclassical home that immediately reminded Kristen of her parents' stately antebellum home above the James River in Richmond. Like her parents' home, it had grounds that were large and sloping and beautifully kept. She could envision her father at this home and it brought a warm feeling to her, brought him closer to her.

Paul put the car into gear and drove through the opened door and down the long circular drive toward the marble steps that led up to the majestic house. Kristen spied a swimming pool to the side of the house and a romantic pool house with a covered veranda close to it.

She couldn't help exclaiming, "Oh Paul, it's beautiful. . . I'm so glad I've come!"

Paul pulled the car to a stop in front of the marble stairs and pointed to the woman who was standing at the top of them. "Be sure to tell your aunt that."

As if she were the heroine in a slow motion film, Kristen turned her head to look at the woman who had commanded so much of her thoughts during the last three months and her eyes widened as she gazed upon her for the first time. Kristen's first thought was that if she had seen her aunt anywhere else in the world, she would have recognized her, for her Aunt Aphrodite was the exact female representation of her father. And her second thought was how this woman could easily have been a southern aristocratic lady. Her bearing was regal, her expression grand, history and tradition were both worn comfortably by her.

With American impulsiveness, Kristen opened the door of the car, and with feet that seemed to have wings on their heels she sped up the stairs to the woman, and to the hands which were extended in welcome. Kristen took ahold of her aunt's hands and was surprised by their strength which was contrary to the small woman's fragile appearance.

And they smiled at one another.

Kristen noticed how her aunt's eyes crinkled at the corners just as her father's had when he smiled and she couldn't help but feel as though somehow, in her aunt's face, she was being given the gift of seeing her father again.

"Christina. . .my dear child. . .welcome home. . ." Aunt Aphrodite spoke in a voice that quivered slightly with age and emotion.

"Oh, aunt. . .I'm so happy to be here. . ." Kristen leaned down and hugged the slight frame of the older woman and was surprised when her aunt turned her face and kissed her. Not a European kiss of a peck on both cheeks but a kiss of love, of joy for the return of a beloved family member. Kristen's eyes caught Paul's over her aunt's shoulders as he came up the stairs.

She smiled at him, a smile of happiness, of contentment,

a smile of coming home.

He winked back at her. He was glad, very glad, to see that the woman he loved like a mother and the woman he loved as a woman were happy in their discovery of one another.

nine

Aunt Aphrodite finally pulled back. "Let me look at you," she said as her deep blue eyes, eyes that had lost none of their clarity through illness and age, and eyes which were indeed as blue as Kristen's father's had been, scanned her face.

Kristen laughed. "I'm afraid you won't find much in me that reminds you of my father."

"Ah. . .but that's not true." Aphrodite spoke softly, her accent more English than Greek and melodious in tone.

"It's true, you don't look like him physically," her blue, blue eyes roamed over Kristen's face, "but in a million other ways you resemble him. In the way your eyes open wide and in the way you tilt your head to the side." She looked down the length of Kristen's body and smiled. "Even in the way your left foot points off to the side when you stand."

Kristen laughed with pleasure. Her aunt described some of her father's characteristics perfectly. For her aunt to have remembered them through all the years of separation told more than any number of words ever could just how often she had thought of her brother.

"Yes, my dear child. . ." she finished her inspection of Kristen. "You look like your father in lots of little ways that speak of heredity without being overt."

Kristen smiled back at her. "Well, you definitely look like your brother. . ." Kristen whispered and was rewarded with a bright smile.

"Yes. . .Nick and I always did look alike. Photos of us as babies are identical and of course, he was many years younger than I so—" she paused because of emotion, "I remember him as a chubby babe."

"I've never seen any photos of my father when he was a

baby or when he was a child for that matter." Kristen wanted to relieve the emotion of the moment.

Aphrodite took her hand. "You will soon, my dear. You will soon. But first, I want you to meet my very dear friend." She turned to the silver-haired man who had stood off to the side watching the exchange between long-lost aunt and niece. "James. . .it's my niece, Christina. . .at last." The older woman breathed out as if she had been holding her breath for a very long time, and James put a supporting arm around Aphrodite's shoulder as he held out his other hand in greeting to Kristen.

"My dear," he turned one of the kindest set of eyes Kristen had ever seen to her, "we are very happy to finally meet you. I'm James Windsor."

"Mr. Windsor. . ." Kristen took his hand and was reminded of the stable friendship of her Uncle George and she liked James Windsor immediately.

"No, please. . .call me James." Kristen nodded her assent as he continued with an admonishing glance at Aphrodite, "but shouldn't we be calling you 'Kristen' rather than 'Christina'?"

Kristen was pleased that he asked but waved all protest aside.

"No, really. . .I don't mind." She turned to Paul. "Paul explained how my name is derived from a long list of Christinas . . .I'm honored to share my grandmother's and my other ancestor's name."

Her response pleased Aphrodite who smiled at her before turning to Paul. The look she gave to Paul was one of a beloved mother to a beloved son, and Kristen knew that the love Paul possessed for his godmother was indeed returned, in full.

"And how are you, dear boy?" she asked softly and reached out her hand to bring him closer to her.

Paul bent down and kissed her on both cheeks. "I'm fine, Nona."

Concern showed in his eyes. "And you?"

She laughed, a much deeper and fuller sound than Kristen would have thought possible to come from such a small body. "James is making sure I don't overdo and that I take all my medication."

She turned to Kristen and taking her by the arm led her into the foyer, "I hate taking medicine. I hate even more being sick."

Then back to Paul she tossed, "Congratulations on the merger, dear boy. That's quite a coup."

"I learned from a pro," Paul said and glanced over at James, who smiled. The respect the two men felt for Aphrodite was obvious and Kristen felt very blessed that such a woman was her aunt.

The foyer was exquisite with brown marble flooring polished to a mirror finish and high windows that let in the afternoon light. The furniture was Italian antique and continued into the living room. One thing that struck Kristen was the lack of carpets. She was just about to ask about that when her eyes were caught by a painting on the wall which was spotlighted by a stream of sunlight pouring onto it from the outdoors. A soft gasp escaped her.

"What is it, my dear?" Aphrodite asked, but then understood when Kristen crossed over to the painting.

It was a small painting, but the mark of its artist was obvious.

"My father told me about this painting. . .he loved El Greco's work. He told me that he had seen it. . .he just forgot to mention that he had seen it in his parents' home," she finished wryly.

"Actually. . .he forgot to mention that he bought it. It was his painting," Aphrodite stated and Kristen, wondering if she detected a note of resentment or condemnation in Aphrodite's voice, turned sharply to her aunt. But one look at the older woman's face relaxed Kristen's fears and she knew that what she had defensively thought of as condemnation was actually only a wistful quality, a longing for something that wasn't, and now could never be.

"Didn't he tell you anything about his life here?" Aphrodite asked and sat in a chair that looked like it knew Aphrodite's body well.

Kristen shrugged her shoulders. She knew that the past had to be faced, she just didn't know if she wanted to face it now.

The events of the last few days, the excitement of finally meeting her aunt, plus jet lag were weighing heavily on her and she suddenly felt exhausted. "Well, of course he told me that he grew up in Greece but. . .I guess I should have asked more questions. My parents and I were very close and well. . .I guess we were enough for one another. The past never seemed to come up." She looked again at the painting. She knew that her father had come from a wealthy family, but until this moment, she hadn't realized just how wealthy. "I guess. . .I was very naive."

"No, not naive, dear child," Kristen looked back at her aunt and was relieved to find no blame in her, "just young."

Kristen thought she heard the voice of experience talking and after giving the painting one more glance walked over to sit in the chair facing her aunt.

Aphrodite continued. "We're all young and we all make mistakes because of our youth. It's simply a reality of life and the sooner people realize that, the happier they will be." Her gaze went past Kristen and Kristen thought it even went past the confines of the four walls, as the older woman seemed to look deep into the past. Both joy and pain flitted across Aphrodite's face as she looked into a past that was bridged with the present by the arrival of Kristen.

"Unfortunately though," she suddenly seemed to remember Kristen and continued, but with bitterness putting an edge on her words, "sometimes, our mistakes haunt us for many years." She looked intently at Kristen, so intently that Kristen felt a bit uncomfortable. "That's when naivete is to be feared."

"Now, Aphrodite," James interjected, "the child is here, you no longer have to concern yourself with all of that. Heed your own words of a moment ago," he gently commanded and Kristen knew that what Paul had said on the plane was right. James probably was the only one who could ever sway Aphrodite.

"My words!" She looked reprovingly at James, but with deep affection, like a partner in a long-lasting marriage might look at the other. "You know very well, James, that I was only repeating the words you have spoken to me time and time again." She laughed, a deep clear sound without any sarcasm attached to it.

"Then heed what I say. You might be a couple of years older than me, but I have reached quite a stately age myself and have learned a few things in all these years," he glanced over at Kristen and smiled, a smile of comradeship.

Kristen returned his smile and at the same time was caught by a yawn. She covered her mouth with her hand and shook her head, embarrassed. "I'm sorry. . .I guess jet lag has caught up with me."

Aphrodite suddenly stood. "Dear me, what sort of a hostess am I? Let me show you to your room and I'll have a plate of refreshments sent up to you. You must be exhausted."

Kristen stood and smiled as she tried to repress another yawn.

"The last few days have been rather. . ." she looked over at Paul and smiled, "eventful."

"It's not every day you discover a long-lost aunt," Paul commented carefully and smiled back at her. But his eyes told her that he understood that finding Aphrodite was just one of the many wonderful events to which she was referring.

Aphrodite stretched out her skinny arms, one reached for Paul, the other for Kristen. "Well, I am a very happy old lady to have the two of you together. As Paul probably told you, I never had children of my own," she paused, "but I feel as though God has blessed me in the two of you. My godson," she looked at Paul, "who has always been like a—son to me," she turned to Kristen, "and my niece, who I have always loved because. . .you are my brother's child."

She hugged them both close to her in the fierce sort of way older people have, as if with age she had learned the secret of time, that it passes so fast that all must hold tightly to those whom they love. "I love you both as if you were my very own children."

Paul looked over his nona's head to Kristen and motioned with his eyebrows that now might be a good time to say something to the older woman about their love for one another. But some instinct warned Kristen that he shouldn't say anything. She minutely shook her head. As far as Kristen was concerned nothing had changed since meeting her aunt. She still felt as though she needed time to get to know her without anything to complicate the process. Kristen was thrilled over her welcome. It was everything and much more than she had ever thought to receive from her aunt. But just because Aphrodite loved them like her children, that didn't necessarily mean that she wanted them involved with one another. . .not yet at any rate.

"Come," Aphrodite let go of Paul's arm but kept ahold of Kristen's as she guided her into the hall and to a door which looked to Kristen as though it might be a closet. She was surprised when Paul opened it.

"An elevator!" Kristen exclaimed.

"My father had it installed for my mother after Nick—" the older woman closed her mouth on the rest of the sentence but Kristen understood what she had left unsaid and finished it for her.

"After my father left?" she asked softly and Aphrodite nodded.

"My mother missed him very much. She was never the same after he left."

"Oh, Aunt Aphrodite. . .I'm so sorry. I don't know what happened in the past, but I'm so sorry that it happened."

"Dear child. . ." Aphrodite reached up and touched Kristen's face. "All of that. . .has nothing to do with you. Nick and I. . . well. . .we finally realized that we were victims of circumstances. . ." She suddenly smiled at Kristen. "But you and I have time to talk. . .I promise that I will tell you all that I can but. . .slowly. . .over the next several days. . ." She looked suddenly sad but even more, old, to Kristen. "It's just too much to talk about all at one time. . .too many people's lives were. . . upset by. . .those events. . ."

"Thea. . ." Kristen whispered the Greek word for "aunt" which Paul had taught to her while on the plane and was rewarded by a wondrous look that replaced the sadness of the moment before. "All of that can wait. It's enough that I'm here with you and that we get to know one another."

"Dear girl. . .my brother and my sister-in-law were indeed blessed to have had you for a daughter," she said, and guiding Kristen into the elevator was about to press the button when Paul stopped her.

"Kristen. . .I'll probably be busy for several days, but I'll call you later." At Aphrodite's rather sharp look Paul was momentarily taken back. He addressed his godmother, a slight challenge in his voice, and as he did so he realized just how wise Kristen was to have suggested that they wait to tell the older woman about their relationship.

"Surely you don't mind if I show your niece around Athens, Nona?"

The older woman seemed to consider it for a moment, and Kristen saw something, like a shadow of fear, cross the older woman's eyes, before she shook it away and smiled. "Of course not. I think that would be very nice as long as," she paused and with a look of authority continued, "you remember that Kristen is my niece and that you are my godson. In the eyes of the church, that is as good as being my son and would make you two cousins."

This startled Kristen and she looked quickly at Paul to see his response. She was a bit relieved to see that he didn't seem to be in the least bit disturbed by her aunt's warning.

Paul smiled. "Don't worry. I won't forget that she is your niece. She will be safe with me." He kissed the older woman, winked at Kristen, and the door closed before Kristen could say another word to him. After traveling with him for so many hours, more than a day, she felt incomplete not to have him beside her, as if a part of her was missing.

She turned and looked at her reflection in the mirror which made up the back wall of the little elevator. Aphrodite met her gaze in the mirror. Her cool, blue eyes collided with Kristen's soft emerald ones.

"You like Paul." It was a statement, not a question. And a

statement that Aphrodite didn't seem too happy about making.

Kristen's lips turned up in a smile. "I'm glad you sent him for me for. . .I like. . ." the elevator stopped and Kristen pushed open the door and with a gentle squeeze, brought her aunt closer to her, "being here with you."

With a smile, a thoughtful smile that didn't quite reach the blue of Aphrodite's eyes, the older woman stepped out of the elevator and guided Kristen down the light and airy hall. As Kristen walked by her side, she was relieved that her aunt didn't ask her anything else about Paul.

The room she showed Kristen was enchanting. Lit by the late afternoon sun, it had high windows and ceilings and Kristen felt as though she had stepped back into Victorian times. It was decorated with muted shades of blue and rose. Fresh flowers were on the dresser and on the round table by the armchair. The bed was a four-poster and high with a lace covering to match the curtains at the window.

"This used to be my room. . .when I was a child and up to about your age," Aphrodite said.

"It's lovely." Kristen spied a huge eucalyptus tree swaying with the breeze outside the open windows. It seemed to be a part of the room, graceful and feminine and timeless, like the room.

Her eyes moved from the outside to the wall between the two windows. It was covered with reminders of people of the past. Portraits, at least half a dozen of them, covered the wall. Some were big, some were small, but all were framed in gold or silver and all were lovingly taken care of. Kristen walked over to the wall.

"Our ancestors." Aphrodite answered Kristen's unvoiced question.

Goosebumps covered Kristen's arms. She rubbed them and thought how she hadn't had so many goosebumps in her life as she had had during the last week. . .since meeting Paul. She pointed to the one in the middle which, from the manner in which the people were dressed, looked like the oldest one. A couple with a baby perched on the father's knee smiled with their eyes from the old canvas. The woman seemed to be holding her hands in a way so that the painter could capture the light in the ring, a very big circular ring, that was on her finger, and Kristen felt certain that she was looking at the hero and heroine of the ring of love.

"They are the founders of our family's shipping business." Aphrodite confirmed Kristen's thought. "That portrait was done shortly after Paul, your great-great-grandfather returned from a very dangerous shipping venture. If he had failed in that journey, or died, as he almost did, then our family would not have been what it became."

"The path of life. . ." Kristen was surprised to hear herself whisper the words out loud and even more surprised to hear Aphrodite respond to them.

"Exactly."

Kristen turned to her. "Do you believe that there is a path of life?"

"I believe," the older woman paused and took a deep breath, "that God knows what our path is but that it is up to us to find it and to follow it."

"Oh, Thea. . ."

"Just like. . ." Aphrodite continued, her eyes moist, "I think that it was a part of your 'path' to come here and to be with me. Thank you, dear, for coming."

"Oh, Thea," Kristen leaned down and kissed the age-softened cheeks. "Thank you."

"Now, I will leave you," she pointed to the wall of portraits and smiled, "with our ancestors." She walked toward the door and paused just before closing it. "Christina. . .I have always wanted a daughter. . .to love. You, as my niece, are that person."

Kristen watched in wonder as the door closed softly behind the rustle of her only living relative. And she smiled.

And later, after eating a dish of fresh fruits—grapes, cantaloupe, and figs—with an assortment of Greek cheeses, Kristen's eyes closed while gazing at the pictures of the men and women who made up her blood. And as the cicadas sang

in the branches outside her window, and the breeze gently
swayed the eucalyptus in time with them, and the red sun
gave way to a silvery moon, she dreamed of Christina and
Paul, of Kristen and Paul, and of the God who directed them
all through time.

ten

The days passed for Kristen and her aunt as summer days of warmth and harmony are meant to pass. It was a time of discovery for the two ladies, a time of learning, a time of telling, a time of deepening friendship. But more than this it was a time of just being, of being together, and of sharing their lives with one another without any interference from the past or from the present.

Of silent accord, the two women kept away from subjects of the past that could hurt and they dwelt instead on telling one another about the happy times. Aphrodite told Kristen about her childhood summers spent in the cool mountains of Greece back in the days when threats of malaria kept people with means away from its lowlands, and she told Kristen about learning French and the French governess she had had as a child who smelled of garlic and wine, old books and velvet.

Kristen, for her part, told her aunt all about her life in Virginia. Summers spent on the Atlantic coast, fall shopping trips to New York with her parents, Christmases in Williamsburg, and springtime strolling about the bountiful and flowerful dogwood groves above the James river.

Paul kept his word and except for a daily phone call to check on her and give her a dosage of love over the phone, he stayed away from Villa Vasilias. James too, even though he stayed at the villa when in Greece, kept away from the two women. But he would watch occasionally from a hidden spot behind a window or from a bench among the pine grove and be glad to see his best friend, Aphrodite, happy with her niece, and Kristen, whom he was coming to admire more and more with each passing day, happy with her aunt. James knew, perhaps even more than Paul, how important it was for

Aphrodite to meet her brother's child. It was a need that had extended through the entire life of the child, now a grown woman, and further beyond.

For days, Kristen was content to walk the large grounds of the villa by her aunt's side and to sit and drink iced coffee and eat baklava and plates of scrumptious fresh fruit with her aunt under the shade of the house's many verandas. She felt as though time had stopped or even gone back to a more gracious era of living.

In the neoclassical home, with the silent staff around to take care of everything, and with her aunt to talk to, who seemed to know a lot about most everything, Kristen could almost imagine herself in Victorian times. They were cut off from the world; Kristen's reclusive life and demanding job in California now seemed like a distant memory.

She had called Lottie the first day she was there only to discover that she had been sent on an archaeological expedition to Santorini, the ancient island of Thera. Kristen had left a message and even though she wanted to see her friend, she had to admit to being glad that it hadn't been immediately upon arrival. She had time to get acquainted with her aunt and. . .to read the Bible Lottie had sent to her in California.

Kristen spent every afternoon, siesta time, when the old mansion was as hushed and as quiet as only the dawning of a new day is in America, poring through the Bible, as both owner and staff slept away the worst of the afternoon heat. After reading the Books of Genesis and Exodus, she'd skipped over to the New Testament. There was much she didn't understand but then again, much that she did, and the greatest revelation of all was coming to the understanding that Jesus was not only God's Son but God Himself. Somehow, she had missed that truth throughout her twenty-eight years that she was of the Christian faith on all official forms. Understanding it and learning it made her feel first amazement, then confusion, but then acceptance brought a clear understanding of the words printed in red, the words spoken by Jesus Himself in the first four books of the New Testament, and she knew that it could only be the truth that Jesus was not only the Son of God but God Himself.

Finally, even though her days were all and more than summer days should be, the August morning came when the past and the present could not be put off anymore than could the Meltemia which started blowing with the dawn of that day. Just as the cool north wind from Russia blew south in order to fill the vacuum created by the hot air rising above the Sahara desert to the direct south of Greece, so Aphrodite's past had to be told in order to fill the vacuum left in Kristen's present. The time of grace, the honeymoon period of getting to know one another, was past, and the two women recognized it when the subject turned naturally to the past which had kept them apart for more than two and a half decades.

Aphrodite had had a glass screen installed on the northern side of the veranda when she saw that the Meltemia was blowing, but when a chair toppled over in the strong wind, she laughed, her deep laugh which Kristen had grown so fond of during the last few days, and said, "Oh my, if it's a 'chair' wind here, imagine how the wind must be blowing on the islands of the Aegean—must be at least a 'table' wind, or maybe even a 'bell' wind."

Kristen got up and set the chair right. "A 'what' wind?"

"That's how the islanders classify the strength of the Meltemia."

Aphrodite explained. "It's either a 'chair' wind, a 'table' wind or a 'bell' wind, depending on what it causes to knock over or in the case of the bell, to ring."

Kristen laughed. "That's adorable."

"As long as you're not on the sea it's adorable. If you're on a ship, or heaven forbid, on a small boat, these gales can be dangerous."

"Thea. . . ?" Kristen wanted to ask about the estrangement between her father and her aunt now but wondered if, like a boat caught in the Meltemia, it might be too dangerous a question, dangerous to their relationship, dangerous to her aunt's health, to ask.

But her aunt was not to be put off. She seemed to know the direction Kristen's thoughts had taken. "What is it, my dear?" she softly prompted.

Kristen ran her tongue over her wind-dried lips and started carefully, "I know we haven't said much about. . .what happened to cause such a rift between you and my father. . ."

The older woman nodded in agreement and surprised Kristen by standing. "It's time." She was subdued, but Kristen was glad to see that the subject didn't seem to bother her. "Let's go into the house. This wind," another chair toppled over, lending credibility to her words, "is a bit too strong for me today."

In the living room Aphrodite closed the doors, something she hadn't done before, and crossing over to her favorite chair, she sank gratefully into its folds. "I don't know how much you know."

"Only what Paul told me." For the first time in days, Kristen worried the gold chain around her neck as she told her aunt the extent of her knowledge. "That there was an argument between my father and my grandfather. But. . .what was the argument about? I have no idea."

Aphrodite took a deep breath. "The argument was because of your mother."

"My mother!"

Aphrodite nodded. "I hate to admit it but your grandfather simply didn't like the fact that your father had married your mother."

"What?" In all the months since Kristen had learned about her aunt and the estrangement between her and her father, she had never imagined anything so. . .so. . .unlikely.

"Your grandfather was a very good businessman," Aphrodite continued. "But. . .he had his failings in other areas. . ." Her voice trailed off as she seemed to look into the past and remember some of those failings.

"But. . ." Kristen was aghast by the idea that someone, her very own grandfather, didn't like her mother. "My mother was a lovely woman. How could somebody not like her? Everyone liked her," she finished simply.

Aphrodite smiled, a sad smile that touched Kristen's heart. "I know. . .I met your mother. . .and I thought she would make the perfect sister-in-law. . .the perfect sister. . ." There was a wistful quality to her tone.

"You met my mother? I didn't know that."

"Yes." That faraway look returned to Aphrodite's eyes. "When your father brought her here to meet us shortly after they were married, I met her. . .right here in this very room." She motioned with her hand. "She was sitting on the chair you are sitting on now and your father was standing by her side and my mother. . ." her voice trailed off and she visibly shook herself. She looked back at Kristen and spoke almost crisply as if that was the only way she could allow herself to remember. "Your mother was a lovely, gracious woman both physically and spiritually."

"So why didn't my. . .grandfather," Kristen almost choked over the word, "like my mother?"

Aphrodite stood and walked over to the mantle. Her steps were sure but her shoulders had lost some of their straightness. She was stooping just a little, as if the weight of remembrance was pushing her down, and remembering the heart attack the older woman had recently recovered from, an alarm went off in Kristen's head. She ran to her aunt's side and gently touched her arm.

"Thea. . .never mind. It's in the past. What's important is that I am here with you now and that you and my parents were reconciled to one another."

"Darling child." She touched Kristen's face, appreciating her concern. "Don't worry. I won't push myself. But I think . . .it's good for me to tell you the story, too. I don't want there to be any misunderstandings between us."

Kristen nodded and led the older woman back to her chair. "Fine. But you must stay seated and promise me that you will stop if it bothers you to retell it."

Aphrodite sat, nodded, and continued. "You have to understand that it wasn't your mother herself that my father objected to. If my father had bothered to take the time to look at your mother, really look at her and get to know her, he would have loved her, I'm sure. The problem was. . .she was a foreigner. She wasn't Greek."

"I see. . ." Kristen said carefully but she wasn't at all sure that she did see.

"Like so many people the world over, my father was prejudiced. Oh, he didn't mind other people from other lands as friends, partners, classmates, etc. . .he wasn't as bad as many. However, he did *not* want his children marrying anyone who wasn't of Greek blood."

"And my mother was an American. . ."

"And. . .even worse. . .already married to your father."

"Worse?" Kristen couldn't understand how that made it worse.

Aphrodite nodded. "By that act, your parents had taken away my father's patriarchal right of giving his permission for his only son," she waved her arm around to include the opulent house, "and heir, to marry."

"But. . .if they were already married, why didn't your father understand that he couldn't do anything about it and just accept the marriage?"

"Because," she touched Kristen's face as she knelt next to her chair, "of the mentality of that time. It was a time when the father's word was the law of the family, no matter how old the children were. According to the way my father thought, your father and mother broke that law."

Kristen shook her head, trying to understand. "A different time entirely."

"Other than that, your parents weren't married in the Greek Orthodox Church, so as far as your grandfather was concerned the marriage was not even an actual fact. At that time, neither he nor the church would recognize any other marriage."

Kristen's eyes widened. "You mean, he tried to tell my mother that she wasn't married?" Kristen never knew a more moral woman than her mother so she knew how painful that must have been to her parents.

"Exactly."

They were silent for a moment, each deep within her own thoughts.

So much of what Aphrodite said explained Kristen's parents and their attitude toward one another to her. That Kristen's father had been devoted to her mother and her mother to her father was practically legendary in Richmond.

"But there's more. Are you sure that you want to hear it?" Aphrodite asked and lightly placed her hand on Kristen's shoulder.

Kristen nodded up to her.

"My father demanded that your father send your mother away, never to see her again or else. . .he would totally disown him and," she paused and squeezed Kristen's shoulder, "all his heirs."

"You mean. . ." Kristen chose her words slowly and carefully, "it was my grandfather. . .who caused the estrangement. . .not my father. . . ?" Kristen now realized that this is what had bothered her the most about the estrangement— thinking that her father had turned his back on his family when they had wanted him.

"Oh yes," Aphrodite answered quickly. "Your father begged him to reconsider. Your grandmother pleaded as well." That faraway look came into her aunt's eyes again. "And when I realized that your father had told my father. . ." she reached out and ran her fingertips softly over Kristen's face, with all the love and longing she felt for her niece in the movement, "that. . .you, my dear. . .were on the way. . .and . . .when. . .*my* father didn't care. . ." Tears gathered in the older woman's deep blue eyes, making them shine in spite of her sadness. She took a deep breath and dabbed at her eyes with her linen handkerchief, "Well, your father took your mother. . .and his unborn child. . .that is you, my dear. . .and left. Never to return."

From somewhere outside, the coo of a pigeon sounded and then the answering sound of its mate and Kristen considered all that her aunt had said. She was glad, more glad than she

could recount, that her father had tried to avoid the estrangement. She was amazed to consider that her grandfather, one
of the ancestors on the wall in her room, hadn't wanted her.
That hurt, but more for the old man than for herself. For
someone to be so blinded by a sense of self-worth because of
race, so blinded that he could hurt so many lives, his own and
others, deserved, in Kristen's opinion, nothing more than her
pity. And that's what Kristen felt for the man. To even consider that Nick would send his Jane back was the greatest
mistake her grandfather could have made. For Kristen's father
had been devoted to her mother all their lives, and it was
almost a blessing that they had passed on together.

But one question bothered Kristen still and looking at her
aunt, she was hesitant to ask, but she knew that she had to, so
that the past could hopefully be left far behind them where it
was meant to be. "But Thea. . .why were you and my father
estranged? You didn't agree with your father, did you?"

"Of course not," she held out her hands helplessly. "But I,"
she paused and the sadness and shame of that time made her
strong voice sound weak, almost frail, "I. . .made the mistake
of. . .remaining silent."

"But why?"

"I. . ." A knock at the door interrupted her. With her strong
voice again in place she asked, "Yes?"

Kristen was surprised to see both James and Paul standing
at the door. "Are we interrupting anything?" James asked as
Paul's eyes found Kristen's where she was still kneeling by
her aunt's chair and immediately understanding that something was amiss, asked with a tilt of his head if she was okay.

Kristen nodded imperceptibly that she was fine and stood as
Aphrodite invited them in. "You are interrupting, but. . .you
are also most welcome to come in."

Seeing Paul again after so many days made Kristen's heart
feel light and happy in spite of the emotionally draining conversation she and her aunt were having. She wanted to run to
him, be close to him, tell him everything, but she somehow
sensed how detrimental to her relationship with her aunt that

would be, especially at this critical time. Instead she smiled at him and walking over to the sofa, she sat down.

James took Kristen's place and stood by Aphrodite's chair. Kristen couldn't help thinking he looked like a cocker spaniel guarding his mistress.

Aphrodite reached up and took her friend's hand. "Kristen and I were just discussing the past." At James's quick look Aphrodite assured him, "I'm fine. It's good for me." She looked over at Kristen and smiled. "It's good for both of us."

Kristen returned the smile. "But, please. . .you don't have to say anything else. Knowing that my father didn't want the estrangement is the most important thing about the past that I needed to know."

"But don't you want to know why I remained silent?"

Kristen nodded yes and from the corner of her eye she noticed how Paul's attention was thoroughly caught. "But only if. . .you want to tell me. . .and if it's not too much for you."

"I want to tell you."

Kristen nodded and waited.

The older woman gathered her thoughts. "I was stunned by my father's behavior. That he didn't want your mother was one thing that could be explained, not condoned, but explained, as I did a moment ago. But not to want Nick's child. . .not to want his own legitimate grandchild. . .shocked me. I saw a side of my father—" she paused. "Well—from past experience I knew what he was capable of and I was afraid to cross him. . .afraid. . ." her glance, a glance which Kristen could only describe as anguish and fear, fell on Paul, before sliding away to look down at the marble floor which had seen such history.

Kristen softly whispered. "It's okay, Thea. . .it's not your fault—"

"—Your father left." She looked quickly back at Kristen and cut her off. "But he tried to contact my mother and me." Bitterness toward her long-dead father colored her words with pain and a hatred toward the man who had fathered her that she obviously didn't want to feel. "But my father never let me have any of the letters. Never," she repeated. "And I lost all contact with Nick until. . .I read about your wedding."

Wryly, Kristen commented, "so I guess something good did come out of that fiasco."

"Were you actually married?"

Kristen looked at Paul quickly before answering. "Ted. . . married me for money. . .he was killed the day of our wedding . . .our wedding was never consummated So. . .I guess you can't really call it a real marriage at all."

"I see. . ."

But Kristen wasn't ready to let go of the far distant past yet. "Thea. . .I just want to know one thing and then we can let go of the past forever. . ."

Aphrodite looked at her and Kristen thought she saw something close to dread or fear in her eyes.

"Did you explain everything to my father. . .did he understand why you were silent and why he never heard from you?"

Relief seemed to bring color back into Aphrodite's face. "Yes, my dear. . .I told your father everything. . ." she glanced up at Paul and repeated, "everything. . ." Paul frowned at the intensity of his godmother's look and that seemed to clear Aphrodite's expression. She turned back to Kristen. "He forgave me and. . .your mother forgave me. . .and we were looking forward to seeing one another. We had planned on spending the entire summer together sailing around the islands of the Aegean. . ."

Her voice trailed off and James noisily cleared his throat, bringing the discussion to an end. "Right. Well, I think that just about says it all. Shall I order tea?" An especially strong gust of wind shook the living-room window.

Aphrodite placed her hand over her companion's. "I think I would like to go and rest for a while. All this talk about the past has exhausted me."

Fear jumped into James's eyes. "Are you feeling quite well? Should I call the doctor?"

Aphrodite laughed. "Dear James. . .I'm only a bit tired, not sick." She glanced over at Kristen as she stood and smiled. "Believe me, it was worth it."

Kristen walked over to her and hugged the thin shoulders close to her, loving the jasmine scent that was the older woman's own special fragrance. "Thank you, Thea. For telling me," she whispered.

Paul walked up to them. "Well, I'm glad to see my two favorite ladies so happy."

Kristen saw the quick look of confusion that jumped into Aphrodite's eyes and motioned to Paul to be careful. Aphrodite still had no idea of the relationship and Kristen knew instinctively that now was not the time to tell her anything about it.

"My dear nona and my," Paul paused for just a second as he looked at Kristen, "my almost-cousin," he explained and Kristen saw light come back into Aphrodite's eyes.

"And don't you forget it," Aphrodite admonished. "You must treat your," she faltered a bit at the word, "cousin—very nicely, Paul."

"And when do I treat women anything but nicely?" he kiddingly asked.

"Your string of women, don't you mean," she admonished, much as older people often admonish younger ones.

"Well, for today, I've come to ask your niece if she would like to do a bit of sightseeing with me this afternoon."

"Oh, I'd love to!" Kristen answered quickly. "Do you have time?"

"After one more meeting," he glanced at his watch, "which I have to leave for now, I'll be free for the next week to show you the sights and sounds of Athens."

Aphrodite turned suddenly to them and the look that filled the lines of her face could only be described as one of soul-stopping dread, as if she had seen a glimpse of the future and she couldn't abide it.

Paul saw it as well. "Nona. . . ? What is it?"

Aphrodite shook her head but still that look in her eyes held, a look that was now covered with yearning. But for what she was yearning, Kristen had no idea.

"What. . .I'm sorry?" Aphrodite asked.

"You don't like the idea of my showing Kristen around?" He sounded almost hurt and definitely confused.

Aphrodite's lips turned up into a smile, but Kristen saw that it was a smile that didn't quite wipe the dread away from her sharp eyes. "Nonsense. I think that would be very nice." She turned abruptly to James. "Do you feel up to continuing our novel?" To Kristen, she explained, "James loves to read out loud and I love to be read to, so we're the perfect pair."

"I think reading out loud is becoming a lost art," James commented as he escorted Aphrodite from the room.

Kristen and Paul turned to one another after the older couple left and forgetting everything but their need to be together, their arms wrapped around one another and Kristen rested her head against Paul's chest.

"Oh, but I've missed you," Paul whispered into Kristen's ear.

"And I've missed you."

"Now that you and Aphrodite seem to be such good friends," he laughed and squeezed her closer to him, "even to the point that she's worried about you going around with me, I think it's time we give ourselves time to do all the things we've planned."

"Our search. . ." she murmured into the fabric of his shirt.

"Our search," he agreed and rubbed his hands over her back before stepping away from her. "Right now, I have to get to that meeting. I'll be back around six. And then I'm going to take you to a very special place."

"Should I dress up?" Her eyes sparkled in anticipation of their evening together.

"In your best walking shoes and jeans," he said, blew her a kiss, and was gone.

eleven

"Best walking shoes and jeans," Kristen repeated, liking the idea of a date which required such apparel. She hurried over to the window to watch Paul as he walked down the marble steps to his sports car. The wind blew his hair in a wavy mass around his face and when he glanced up and waved, somehow knowing that she was watching him, Kristen felt a lump of pure happiness bubble up inside her. To think that that handsome, wonderful, kind man loved her, Kristen King, was the most amazing thing Kristen could imagine. She waved back and watched until his car disappeared down the tree-lined drive and out onto the main road.

Kristen turned and looked around the room that had seen such drama throughout the years. So far, two of the things which she had searched for in traveling to Greece, finding a blood relative and finding out about the past, had been realized in this room today. She only hoped that her quest with Paul, as they learned about their new and fragile love and their search for that Something More in life which she was now certain had everything to do with God, would be equally successful.

Giving the room one more sweeping glance, somehow feeling not sadness but closeness, because she knew that both her parents had been there, she walked out and was about to head up the stairs to her bedroom when, on an impulse, she decided to look around the library instead. Until Paul came for her at six, she had nothing to do, and she knew that she would be impatient at best. A stroll through the library would help.

Aphrodite had shown Kristen around the library on one of their numerous walks around the house and grounds. The library was her aunt's pride and joy, but James's domain. He lovingly took care of it, even to being the one who dusted its numerous shelves. It boasted several manuscripts dating from the early Christian period and medieval times, and much memorabilia from the first modern Olympics held in 1896 in Athens, which the Vasilias family had helped to organize and finance and even had a family member participate in.

Kristen walked over to a manuscript in a glass case. It was a twelfth-century manuscript written in Greek which told about the conquest of Greece by the invading Franks after the fourth crusader's sacking of Constantinople in 1204. She knew that her college friend, Melissa Gilbert, now Melissa Karalis, was an expert on the subject of medieval Greece and probably knew what treasures the old manuscript held. She had tried calling Melissa several times at her Peloponnesian home but there had been no answer. As Kristen turned away from the treasured book to the next display, a Bible, she made a mental note to try and call Melissa once again.

Running her hand over the glass display case which contained a Byzantine Bible bound in enamel, she wished, like so many others before her, that she could touch the vellum pages of the ninth-century book and she thought how the Byzantine enamel work on its cover was probably as masterful as the little painting by El Greco which hung in the next room.

"Now there's a book I wish I could read!" she whispered longingly. But ancient Greek was a little bit more than she could tackle. At the moment, she was thrilled when she could correctly handle a phrase or two in modern Greek. Sighing, she turned away from the manuscript and started searching among the shelves. In several nooks and crannies, James had set up displays of books he found exceptionally interesting.

Kristen stopped in front of one. Another Bible, old and well-worn, but more from use than age. The oils of loving hands had turned the pages a rich gold along the edges. Carefully, Kristen turned the book to the title page.

It was written in English! And she gasped when she read the inscription. Written in English were the words:

To my dear wife Christina,
   All my love forever and ever,

                                    Your husband,
                                       Paul
                                 Galaxidi, Greece

Kristen felt as if her breath had been knocked out of her. She couldn't believe it, but somehow she had found Christina's Bible! She tried to remember what Paul had told her about the ring of love. Something about the ring having come to symbolize Christina and Paul's love and. . .faith.

Kristen picked the book up and hugged it close to her heart. Now she knew just what their faith had consisted of and how deeply it ran. And. . .Kristen was beginning to realize that she had a lot more in common with her ancestors than just her name and her sudden love for her Paul. Handling the precious book with infinite care, Kristen carried it over to a table by the tall window and slowly, lovingly turned its pages. She let out a cry of delight when she discovered notes written with neat, very small letters in the margins. Even though the notes were written in Greek, it was a link with her ancestors and one which she knew that she and Paul would go over together and cherish.

She started to close the book but it opened of its own accord, as if it had been opened many times at a particular page. Kristen couldn't resist one last peek so she opened it wide.

She let out a gasp of delight when she discovered that it was the Vasilias family's Bible, its Record of Births. It dated from the time of Paul and Christina's birth and ended with an entry recording. . .her own birth. She read:

Christina Vasilias—Born July 20, 1967
     (Richmond, Virginia, U.S.A.)
Daughter of Nick P. Vasilias and Jane Ann Pierce

Kristen sat and looked at that inscription. A tear, a poignant tear of happiness and of sadness, slowly fell from her long lashes to draw a line down her face.

"Christina?" Kristen looked up as her Aunt Aphrodite walked on slippered feet over to her. Seeing the book her niece held she understood her niece's tear. "So. . .you found the family Bible."

Kristen nodded. "I think. . .that this one," she motioned to the book which she held open in her hands, "is worth much more than that one," she looked over toward the Byzantine Bible that sat elegantly behind its burglarproof case.

"There are many different kinds of worth," Aphrodite agreed and sat in the chair next to Kristen. She pointed to the inscription that recorded Kristen's birth. "My mother penned that the very day she found out about your birth. She sat right where you are sitting now and with tears in her eyes said, 'Praise God, my granddaughter has been safely born. I hope someday, Aphrodite, that I can give this book, our family Bible, to her'."

Kristen's eyes opened wide in joy and wonder.

"In my mother's name. . .I present this family Bible to you, dear Christina."

"Oh, Thea. . .I don't know what to say. . ."

Aphrodite continued. "All our ancestors have loved God. . . even my father did. . .at one time. He is the only one who didn't accept God's path for our lives. . .and look what grief his rebellion caused our family. I think. . .I think it had a lot to do with the two world wars and the Greek civil war. . .because he wasn't like that always. . ." she spoke thoughtfully as though she had tried to understand a million times before, "and maybe a lot to do with too much money as well. . .I don't know. . ." She shook her silver head. Confusion was in its movement and Kristen felt a rush of love for this woman who had the blood of Paul and Christina running through her veins just as she did. Taking her aunt's hand, Kristen whispered, "I love you, Thea." It came out naturally and both Kristen and Aphrodite knew that it was true.

"Oh, Christina. . .I love you too, just as. . .your grand-mother, your yiayia, did."

And their arms were around one another in an embrace of acceptance and understanding of the past that had, in spite of the rebellion of one man, been rescued by God to bring them all back together again. As the scent of jasmine wafted in through the opened window to mix with that of her aunt, Kristen thought how the ring of love, not a ring of substance, but the ring formed by God, wound around them gently, lovingly.

The housekeeper softly knocked on the doorjamb, bringing them reluctantly apart.

"Excuse me, ma'am," she addressed Kristen, "but you are wanted on the phone by a Miss Lottie," she said and left.

Kristen jumped out of her aunt's arms. "Oh my. . .Lottie! She must be back!"

"One of the friends you told me about?" At Kristen's happy nod she suggested, "Why don't you take the call in my study?"

Kristen started to get up but then stopped. She looked down at the Bible, her family Bible, and then at her aunt. "Why don't we just leave this book here in the library for now?"

Kristen could tell that her aunt was pleased with the suggestion by the way her eyes crinkled at the corners, just like her father's had when he was pleased. "I'd like that."

"Maybe," Kristen suggested hesitantly, "you should ask James to read it to you." At Aphrodite's surprised look, Kristen continued. "Lottie recently sent me a Bible for my birthday. I've been reading it. . .it's amazing!"

"Maybe I will." Aphrodite laughed her low, forceful laugh. "That is. . .if I can get James to stay awake long enough to read more than two pages."

"Is that what happened now?"

"He's snoring," she confirmed. "But I left him. He's leaving for a few days in England in the morning. At our age—you grab sleep whenever it graces you." She waved her hand. "Now go on with you. Your friend must be wondering what's happened to you."

Aphrodite's words were more than true. Lottie did wonder

what had happened to Kristen, but also what had happened to make Kristen all of a sudden travel to Greece!

"I couldn't believe it when I got your message and they said that you were calling from Athens. What happened? Don't tell me you came to surprise me and then found me gone?"

Kristen laughed and could imagine her little redheaded friend through the wire. Lottie had always reminded Kristen of a miniature sports car of vivacious red coloring that was always trying to pass others and Kristen could tell, as she explained to Lottie about her aunt and Paul and their quest, that that hadn't changed even though she had changed her way of thinking about life.

"Kristen. . .I'm. . .I'm so happy. . .I didn't know how you would react to getting a Bible for your birthday," she laughed, her deep hardy laugh that was so familiar to Kristen, "it certainly is different from the statue I gave to you last year!"

"Oh Lottie. . .I adore the statue. . .but the Bible. . .it gives so much!"

"It's life-giving," Lottie said, and Kristen was amazed to hear Lottie speak of things so deep and philosophical. Previously, she had always jested about people who became "deep and heavy" as she used to call it.

"It's life-giving," Lottie continued, "and absolutely perfect for wherever you are in life."

Kristen nodded into the phone. "Your timing certainly couldn't have been better. . .just when Paul and I were wondering where to start searching for that Something More in life. . .the doorbell rang and the deliveryman handed me your package."

"That's something neat about God's timing, Kristen." She paused. "It's always perfect. . .just trust Him and He will lead you down the path that has been marked out for you since the beginning of time. It's a lot better than the path we mark out for ourselves. . .that's for sure! Look at me! I thought I'd be in Athens during my stay in Greece and suddenly this Santorini find exploded around me. And because I was already in Athens, the position was given to me by the university. It never would have been given to me otherwise. These super finds are too few and far between to be handed to a junior archaeologist."

"And you've always loved things to do with Santorini," Kristen commented, remembering the hours she had listened to Lottie talk about the lost civilization of Atlantis.

"It's what made me go into archeology in the first place. . . who knows. . .maybe I'll find the lost city of Atlantis after all!" She paused and with an inner peace Kristen had never heard in her friend before she continued softly, almost reverently, "but you know. . .it doesn't even matter anymore. . . I've already found the God who was lost to me. . .and that's the most important find I'll ever make."

twelve

After hanging up the phone Kristen thought about her friend and the amazing events in her life and then she was reminded about her other friend, Melissa Karalis.

The events of Melissa's life were amazing, too. Kristen remembered that she had almost married her handsome Greek doctor during their university days, but then, something had happened to split Melissa from Luke just weeks before their wedding. Melissa had changed and from the deep recesses of her mind, Kristen vaguely remembered Melissa as having said something about having discovered that she shouldn't rely on the man she loved to be her savior from all the hurts of the world, but rather, that she had learned that there was One who she could and should rely on. . . .

Kristen shook her head and wondered, *Had Melissa meant God?*

Kristen picked up the phone and again dialed her friend's Peloponnesian home. She really wanted to talk to Melissa and she was thrilled when her efforts were rewarded by the phone being answered this time.

"*Embros.*" A woman's voice answered.

"*Yia Sas.*" Kristen was pleased that she remembered how to say "Hello" in Greek. "Melissa, please. . .*parakalo.*"

Understanding that the caller was English-speaking, the gracious woman answered in English. "Melissa isn't here. She's in Athens in the hospital."

"In the hospital!"

The woman laughed. "Don't worry. Both she and the baby are fine."

"Baby!"

The woman, who Kristen learned was Melissa's sister-in-law, Anastasia, laughed and was delighted to give Kristen all the particulars about the birth of her beloved brother and sister-in-law's baby, even to informing Kristen that the hospital where Melissa was staying was located very close to Kristen's aunt's home.

Kristen asked Anastasia not to tell Melissa that she had called, wanting instead to surprise Melissa in the morning with a visit.

Anastasia was thrilled with the idea and upon putting down the phone, Kristen felt sure that Melissa's sister-in-law, Anastasia, was a good friend to Melissa.

ಜಿ

Paul came and picked Kristen up at precisely six o'clock that evening. She was dressed in the requested jeans and walking shoes and was anxious to tell him all about the wonderful events of the day. As he drove through the quiet streets of Athens, which he told her were only so quiet during the month of August when most Athenians were away on holiday, she quickly and excitedly told him about finding the family Bible, about Aphrodite giving it to her, about her conversation with Lottie, and about Melissa's new baby.

When she'd finished he repeated the words Lottie had finished on.

"God's perfect timing. . .I'm beginning to believe in it."

The depth of feeling he put into the words impressed and surprised Kristen. She waited expectantly for him to continue.

He grinned, as pleased as a stray cat might be who had just found a T-bone steak. "You're not the only one who's been busy discovering new and wonderful things this week."

"What do you mean?"

"Well. . .when I haven't been attending to my job, I've been busy studying and reading the Bible and. . .meeting with Pastor Dean."

"What?"

"Well. . .we did come here to search for that Unknown, Something More, didn't we?" he gently reminded her. "And since we were literally thrown together with the pastor on that beach below your home last week. . ." he shrugged his shoulders, "well, when he called me a few days ago, right after he returned from San Francisco, I told him about our questions and search and. . .we've been meeting every night."

"Paul!" That Kristen was pleased was putting it mildly. She knew that he was serious about searching.

"Kristen," he glanced over at her, "something you have probably guessed about me. . .when I say something or decide to do something, I'm serious about it. And I normally act on it immediately. Our search. . .is very important to me." He stopped at a light and reaching over, took her hand in his. "I think that it is very important to our love. . .one of the reasons our love is going to be the long-lasting kind. . .like Paul and Christina's."

"Oh, Paul. . ." She brought his hand up to her face and rubbed the back of it against her cheek. "I believe so too." After a moment of happy silence Kristen asked, "So. . .what have you learned?"

She was curious about his visits with the pastor.

Paul blew out a deep breath, "So much. . .but the most important thing is—that we are on the right track. The Bible, known as God's Word, is the place to search. I've only read a small part of it, the four gospels—the first four books in the New Testament telling about Jesus' life on earth—and the fifth book, the Book of Acts, which tells about the spreading of Jesus's message throughout the world—and I feel almost certain that God, in the person of Jesus Christ, is that Unknown, Something More that we are searching for."

"Oh, Paul. . .I think so too. I haven't done too much reading but from what I've read and from talking to Lottie. . .I think so too," she repeated simply and felt joy, a joy unlike any she had ever felt before, fill her as the city slid past her window.

Paul left the modern city streets behind and turned onto the quaint small streets that made up the old town of Athens, called the Plaka. The buildings were built right onto the narrow roads and at a couple of points as Paul drove through the roads, careful of strolling tourists, it seemed as though the corners of the old buildings might possibly be clipped by the side of the car.

He drew her attention upward. Kristen gasped. "The Acropolis!" She swiveled around in her seat, cocking her head at an angle and back as far as it would go to see the ancient walls of Athens' High City. "It's right over our heads! Is that where we're going?"

Paul smiled, a smile that said "just you wait and see," and drove up and past the busy tourist section until he reached a quiet lane right at the base of the Acropolis's butte. Trees—pine trees, straight cypress trees, and olive trees—covered the slopes on the left side of the lane for several meters until the cliffs were reached.

He turned to the right and pulled into the driveway of a beautiful neoclassical house, and switched off the car.

And suddenly Kristen realized where they were. "It's your house!"

In all the excitement of the past week, she had totally forgotten about his house.

He led her to the side of the house, which was also the entrance, and to a gate which opened up onto a courtyard that was lovingly tended and filled with orange and lemon trees and with the delicate white blossoms of jasmine filling the courtyard with their sweet scent. Kristen breathed in deeply. "I think I will always associate jasmine with my aunt. . ."

As if suddenly realizing it, Paul answered, "You're right. That is her fragrance."

Kristen smiled indulgently at him before turning her attention to the courtyard. She felt as though she had stepped into another world! Her aunt's house had the feeling of her parent's home. It was a big stately mansion. But Paul's home was something totally different. Swallows played under the eaves of the ceramic roof, bees buzzed busily, wanting to make their way home in the late afternoon sunlight, cicadas still ground their legs as they played their summertime song in the pine grove across the street. . . . It all combined to make Kristen feel as though she were a part of a fairy tale. She half expected Thumbelina to come riding by on the back of one of the swallows.

Kristen turned to Paul. She remembered reading that a person's home told a lot about the personality of a person. Knowing Paul as she did, Kristen knew that this home told clearly about the warm man she had grown to love. It was inviting yet stately, elegant yet cozy, old and yet new. "Paul," her green eyes sparkled out her joy in his home, "your home is enchanting."

He was pleased. "I'm glad you like it. I'd give you a tour but," he glanced at his watch, "if you don't mind, it will have to wait for later."

Kristen looked at him in surprise. "I thought this was it for tonight!"

"My dear Kristen," he looked at her with those same dark eyes that she had wanted to fall into in San Francisco, and she now yearned to wrap her arms around him and to hold him and to love him and to keep him next to her always. He was the most precious person in the entire world to her.

He paused and felt the blood pound in his head as he easily read what was written in her eyes because it was a reflection of his own want, his own desire. But, ignoring his want, her want, he continued, "I don't think I would have asked you to dress so casually if I had only wanted to show you my house." He forced a chuckle and looked down at the smooth marble stones. "Neither the marble out here nor the parquet floors inside require walking shoes." He cleared his throat, respect in his tone. "But for a walking tour up to the Areopagus, the spot from where the Apostle Paul is traditionally thought to have preached to the people of this city, good nonslip walking shoes are a must."

"Oh, Paul, that sounds wonderful," she said, emotion lacing her voice, and she let her arms have their way and wound them around his neck. After a week of holding her emotions at bay, she just had to hold him for one moment.

Paul drew her to him. Their foreheads touched, their heartbeats ran together, and Paul whispered, his accent prominent and sweet with emotion, "I love you, Kristen. There's something very special between us."

Kristen shook her head. "No, Paul. . .I don't think there is something special between us. . ." she smiled. "I think. . .that there is something very special among us. . .and. . .I'm beginning to believe that that special Something. . .is God."

"Kristen. . ." he pulled her closer to him, breathing in the scent that was all her own and sounding to his own ears more like Pastor Dean whom he had spent so much time with that week than himself, he said the unfamiliar words, but words he truly meant, "Praise God, I found you."

Their lips came together in a light kiss of sweet, growing love which promised a future of so much more.

thirteen

Holding hands, Kristen and Paul left his house and walked along the quaint roads that ran in and around the red-roofed buildings huddled picturesquely against the northern slopes of the Acropolis. The roads were actually little more than paths originally laid out in the days when horses and donkeys and human feet were the mode of travel. Cars weren't allowed on most of the roads, so pedestrians of all sizes, and of all nationalities, and of all ages filled the space as people wandered among the nooks and crannies, all enjoying the holiday atmosphere and checking out the many tastefully appointed tourist shops. Grecian urns, replicas of those found in the very location where tourist feet now trod, Greek worry beads, and T-shirts with anything from Plato to the famous Greek cats printed on the front, abounded in the shops.

Several times, young waiters dressed in dark pants and white shirts, tried to escort Kristen and Paul into a rooftop taverns for dinner, something Kristen found charming and that gave her the feeling of being more an honored guest rather than a paying customer. But Paul politely declined in his own language and they moved on.

They skirted the upper slopes of the old town, with the grinding of the cicadas and the cooing of the pigeons accompanying them as they walked, and the ever-present Meltemia blowing everything in a symphony of sound and movement. Sidewalks of steep stairs led down into the gaily lit heart of the Plaka. Like a fair, the streets reminded Kristen of Disneyland and a re-created setting.

But a quick glance above her left shoulder to the majestic ruins of the Acropolis with the massive cyclopean walls dating from the late Bronze Age quickly confirmed that the streets were not a re-creation. They were the real thing, with foundations that went back several millennium.

They left the commotion of the coffee shops and tourist shops and came upon the stone and concrete path, called Theorias Way, that cut through the ancient city of Athens like a pathway into another time. Turning around and around, Kristen sucked in her breath at the view that was before her, behind her, above her, and below her.

"It's beautiful, isn't it?" Paul whispered by her side.

Kristen nodded and thought how "beautiful" didn't go far in describing the view. Above her was the Acropolis sitting ageless and golden, below her was a land of ancient Greek temples and medieval churches, before her was an observatory and a bald, stony hill where people could be seen standing and sitting in the foreground, and behind her was the old town with its mixture of neoclassical buildings built in the protection of the fortress above its head.

"I'm not sure what I'm looking at. . .but it's one of the prettiest sights I've ever seen," Kristen finally breathed out. "I feel as though I've stepped into an epic film and I've gone back in time." She laughed and waved her hand to include all the buildings and constructions that spoke of so many different ages. "But which time period, I'm not sure."

Paul let go of her hand and opened one of the books he was carrying. "Well, how about if we go back to about the time of the Apostle Paul?" he suggested.

"Our quest. . ." Kristen whispered and looked down at the guidebook he held and felt the thrill of discovery shoot through her.

"Our quest," he returned and pointed to a passage in the book. "You see, when the Apostle Paul arrived here in about the year A.D. 51, Athens' golden days were half a millennium in the past and the city," he pointed down to the ancient site below them, "the ancient agora—that is, marketplace—was said to have resembled an outdoor art gallery."

Kristen looked down at the ancient marketplace he indicated and laughed. "What it is now?" Even from about a hundred feet up she could see many statues and columns and altars and walls from ancient buildings filling the grounds. There were even a couple of temples.

Paul smiled. "Ah. . .this is nothing compared to what it was then. The city that was has been destroyed and set on fire many times by invading people—barbarians—that came swarming in from the north after the collapse of the Roman Empire." He squinted into the sun that was about two hours from setting and continued, "When St. Paul visited Athens it was still the most respected center of learning in the world. Plato's University was still in session and the city was filled to capa-city with altars and temples that were in use."

Kristen looked at him in surprise. "Really?"

He tucked her arm under his elbow as they continued to walk slowly down the old path. "I read," Paul motioned to the book he carried, "how the Roman satirist Petronius, who was a contemporary of the Apostle Paul's, wrote that it was easier to find a statue of a god in Athens than a man."

"I wonder how that made St. Paul feel. . ." Kristen wanted to learn all she could about the St. Paul of the Bible.

Paul considered that for a moment before answering, "Well, his background was Jewish, his citizenship was Roman, his learning was influenced by the Greek world, and his thought had become Christian." He paused thoughtfully. "I imagine all the temples and altars that abounded probably offended the Jewish part of him, impressed the Roman part of him, were beautiful to the Greek part of him, and distressed the Christian part of him."

"What an interesting man. . .I didn't realize that he was anything but Jewish," she paused, "and Christian, of course."

"Interesting doesn't go far in describing Paul. He was amazing. To leave his home and travel as he did, bringing new, but true, ideas to a place that had ancient ideas. . .he was not only a very learned man, but a brave one as well." He motioned down at the ancient marketplace and pulled from his back pocket a small New Testament.

"Paul!" Kristen exclaimed. "You've gotten a Bible!"

His eyes twinkled. "I've gotten several Bibles," he corrected and held the little Testament up. "This one goes with me every-where."

Kristen watched him open the book and thought how it added to his stature. *There is something masculine about a man handling a Bible,* she decided, as he opened it to a pre-marked page.

"I want to read to you from this spot what was written about Paul while he was in Athens," he motioned around him at the ancient city St. Paul had visited, "and in a few minutes, I'll read St. Paul's exact words from the location where he most likely spoke them."

Kristen felt tears, tears of wonder, tears of joy, tears of love build up behind her eyes for this man. To say that she admired Paul wasn't enough. And to say that she respected him still wasn't enough. He had something special and, through his research, was acquiring something more every day that seemed to fill him and make him more of a man to be loved and cherished and adored and respected. There was so much more to him than just ambition and wealth and good looks. So much more simply because he knew that there was Some-thing More in life than the empty demands made on men in the late twentieth century and he wasn't afraid to go out and find it.

The pages of the Testament ruffled in the ever-present wind that whipped across the path, and the paper seemed to demand its need to be read. Paul read, deeply, richly of the words. " 'While Paul was waiting for them in Athens,' " he glanced at Kristen and explained, " 'them' being Silas and Timothy, his friends who were to join him, 'he was greatly distressed to see that the city was full of idols. So he reasoned in the synagogue with the Jews and the God-fearing Greeks, as well as in the marketplace.' "

"Marketplace!" Kristen exclaimed and looked down at the ancient site below her. "Do you mean there?"

Paul smiled. "Exactly."

Kristen looked at the site with new eyes. To think that she was looking at the actual place which was written about in the

Bible, the actual site where the Apostle Paul reasoned with the Jews and the God-fearing Greeks, was almost too much for her North American brain to assimilate. She looked at her Paul and hesitantly tried to explain what she was feeling. "Whenever I heard the Bible stories. . .when I was a little girl. . .they almost seemed like they were in fictional lands. . .but right now. . ." she turned and looked down over the ancient site below her, holding her windblown hair away from her face, "I'm looking at the actual place. . .the actual setting. . ." her words trailed off.

"I know what you mean, and I've lived here all my life," he replied in understanding before turning back to the ruffling pages of the Testament and continuing to read, " 'A group of Epicurean and Stoic philosophers began to dispute with him. Some of them asked, 'What is this babbler trying to say?' Others remarked, 'He seems to be advocating foreign gods.' They said this because Paul was preaching the good news about Jesus and the Resurrection. Then they took him and brought him to a meeting of the Areopagus, where they said to him, 'May we know what this new teaching is that you are presenting? You are bringing some strange ideas to our ears, and we want to know what they mean'.''

"I wonder what exactly he was saying to them?" Kristen interrupted.

"When I read to you from the Areopagus what Paul said to the Council of the Areopagus," he pointed to the bald hill that was before them, "I think you'll understand."

"Areopagus? Council of Areopagus?" The words were so foreign sounding to Kristen but the hill wasn't. It was the one that was straight ahead of them and filled with people.

"Known as the Areopagus or Hill of Ares, or by the time Paul arrived during the Roman period, the Hill of Mars, it was the site of the ancient council of nobles called The Council of the Areopagus," Paul explained and looked back down at Kristen. "In Athens' earlier history, it was both the senate and the supreme judicial court for Athens, but by the time of St. Paul's visit the council had authority only in religious and moral issues."

"So. . .it was to this windblown hill that Paul was brought?"

Paul chuckled. "Well. . .they have found evidence of a structure having been there then. . .some sort of public building, I imagine."

"I always thought that he talked to the Athenians from the Acropolis." She motioned to the fortress that was about twice the height of the Hill of Ares and located to the east of it.

"He probably visited there," Paul conceded.

She turned back to the bald, unassuming hill. Somehow she felt drawn to it much more than she did to the world-famous Acropolis with its array of priceless temples and buildings. The wind seemed to be wrapping invisible threads around her and they were pulling her toward the hill's windy heights. She took Paul's hand and started walking along the path toward the stone stairs that led up to the rocky hill.

But Paul stopped her. "Wait." She turned and looked at him with questioning eyes. "Before we go up there and I read the words of St. Paul, I want to read one more thing which I found in the guidebook. I think it will help you to understand his speech better and. . ." he reached out and gently touched her cheek, "it goes along with what we said that first day that we met."

She tilted her head in question. "We said so much that day. . ."

"About. . .that Unknown, Something More. . ."

Slowly, she nodded her head and thought how that invisible thread was now weaving itself around the two of them. "Tell me," she gently commanded and she felt as though she and Paul were the only ones on the path below the Hill of Mars. The sounds of the evening faded into the background and although they were surrounded by humanity, it was as if they were alone. But no, not alone exactly either. Something, Someone was among them.

"There was a Greek traveler and geographer whose name was Pausanius who visited Athens about a century after the apostle. He wrote in detail about everything he saw." Paul grinned. "I guess you could say Pausanius wrote the world's first guidebook. On the road from the port of Phaleron," he pointed off in the direction of the sea, "he reported as having seen. . ." Paul looked down at the book and read, " 'altars of the gods named Unknown'."

"Gods named Unknown. . ." Kristen whispered in awe.

Paul nodded and repeated, "gods named Unknown." He paused, and as he took her hand, they left the path and walked toward the stone stairs that led to the top of the hill. "So you see, Kristen—we aren't the only ones to realize that there is an Unknown, Something More in life than what our world would have us believe. Even in the ancient days which were filled with gods more personally named than ours of money and ambition and success, people knew that there was an Unknown, Something More to life."

Kristen squeezed his hand. Words weren't needed as that invisible thread seemed to wrap them tighter than ever together as they stepped, man and woman, simultaneously upon the bottom stone step that led to the summit of that unassuming hill from where the Apostle Paul was said to have spoken to the Athenians.

Kristen knew that she had learned more on their walk down the path that led to this hill than a month of lectures could have taught her. And some invisible force seemed to be telling her that she was about to learn more than she had learned in a lifetime of questions. She felt certain that the Unknown was about to be made known to her—and to be made known to her beautifully.

It filled her with excitement, excitement and peace.

fourteen

Sixteen stone steps, treacherous steps, old steps, maybe even ancient ones, cut out from the very substance of the hill, led to the top. Kristen counted them, one by one, as she ascended hand-in-hand with Paul and wondered if these were perhaps the very steps St. Paul had used.

If they had thought that the wind along the path had been strong, they realized that it was nothing compared to that at the top of the Hill of Ares. Kristen laughed into it and Paul laughed with her. It was more than exhilarating and more than invigorating. It was welcoming and somehow right, as if doldrums would have been all wrong and too tame for the hill that had heard the words spoken by that mighty man of God 1,900 years before the current world's population was born. The wind seemed to hold the words of the apostle in its age-less movement, in its whistling tune. They both felt it, they both loved it, and they were both anxious for Paul to read the actual words which St. Paul had spoken about the Unknown God from this very spot on earth.

At the top, Paul led Kristen over the jagged and slippery rocks and around people who sat upon smoother ones, to the gravelly section on the western side. There they found a stone and sat to look out over the city that sprawled outward to the mountains that encircled it on three sides and to the sea that hung like a sapphire from around its neck to the south. A fairy wind danced around Kristen's feet and a plastic bag, a sad leftover from somebody's picnic, was caught by the wind and pushed against a wild artichoke bush. Paul kicked it away from the thorny, purple flower with his foot and balling it up, stuffed it in his pocket to throw away later. A plastic bag was all wrong for what they had come to do.

That invisible thread, that which Kristen had felt on the

pathway leading to the hill, seemed to bind them tighter and tighter as the wind encircled them. Kristen held tightly to Paul's arm. She loved this moment in time, she anticipated the next, and she hoped that the feeling she now possessed, the feeling of being on the brink of a wonderful discovery, would never leave her even after the discovery was made. Paul leaned closer to her as he reached into his back pocket for the little Testament.

"Can't you just imagine that St. Paul spoke on a day such as this one?"

Kristen looked out over the scene before her. Clouds danced in the sky above, swallows played in the wind all around, and the city, the beautiful and sprawling modern city of Athens hummed like an electrical wire below them. The people of the city seemed too busy to hear even itself, much less something as simple, but as magnificent, as words. But then, looking around her at the summit of the hill, Kristen was moved to realize that people, people representing cities and countries and continents from the world over seemed to have converged on the summit of Mars Hill. Black and white, yellow and red, tall and short, fat and skinny, old and young people were all atop the hill and were all somehow subdued, as if they too had journeyed to this spot to quest after something, something that only this spot on earth was meant to hand to them, a gift free of charge.

Looking closer at the people, Kristen drew in her breath and Paul turned to her in question.

"Look," she pointed. Many of the people seemed to hold books such as the one Paul now held opened to the seventeenth chapter of Acts.

"Bibles," Paul whispered and looked back at her with an expression of such tenderness and wonder that Kristen felt tears form at the back of her eyes. "Obviously. . .others feel . . ." he breathed in deeply, "what we feel, Kristen."

"Oh, Paul. . ." she laid her head against his shoulders and was just enjoying the moment of revelation, of understanding that there were many other people in the world who were interested in searching for that wonderful Something More in life when her eyes were caught by such an extraordinary sight that she was sure it must be a figment of her imagination.

A man, dressed in the long billowing robes of Biblical days, with sandal-clad feet, appeared like an apparition from the west side of the hill.

Kristen blinked her eyes. If she had been asked to describe St. Paul as he might have been when he visited the Hill of Ares, she would have described him exactly as this man appeared. Robes flowing in the wind, red hair licking out behind him like a flame in the evening sky, and eyes, crinkled eyes that were kind, and yet disturbed for the intelligent people to whom he wanted to make known the Unknown God, would have belonged to St. Paul as they did to this man.

"Paul?" she whispered to her Paul and squeezed his arm. But she didn't have to say anything. Her Paul had seen the man and from the whispered commotion which she heard coming from behind her and around her, Japanese spoken to her right, Spanish to her left, Greek all around, and a multitude of English-speaking accents that must have covered at least four continents, Kristen knew that all the people on the hill, people representing the entire world, had seen the man.

"I don't believe it," Paul whispered.

"Neither do I."

The man, short of height and small in size, but seemingly bigger than life, stopped about ten feet from Kristen and Paul and with his back to the Acropolis, took a silent moment to gaze out over the city, over the world it represented. He closed his eyes and, as the real apostle might have done all those ages ago, he very obviously offered up a silent prayer for Athens and the people she contained.

When he opened his eyes, he looked directly at Kristen and Paul and smiled slightly, before encompassing all the people on the hill with the brilliance of his gaze. As he looked from face to face, all the languages that were spoken on that hilltop fell silent as the people gathered around the man. Kristen thought how they were all spokes of a wheel, while the man was the hub.

"Men of Athens!" the man's voice boomed out and Paul, a modern day man of Athens, understood immediately what this man dressed as St. Paul was about to do.

He put his arm around Kristen's shoulder and squeezing her close to him, said with the excitement he felt lacing his voice, "Kristen. . .he's going to recite St. Paul's speech!"

Kristen looked at her Paul in amazement, her green eyes flashing in wonder. "Are you sure?"

"Listen," Paul instructed and trained his eyes back on the St. Paul. Kristen did the same.

The man continued, his voice clear and powerful and yet, with a love-sweetened sound that travelled with the wind to the hilltop's waiting ears. "I see that in every way you are very religious. For as I walked around and looked carefully at your objects of worship, I even found an altar with this inscription: *To An Unknown God.*"

Kristen grabbed ahold of Paul's free hand and squeezed it. *To An Unknown God!* The words reverberated within her brain.

With caring and yet with challenge in his tone, the man, the wonderful man who cared enough to dress as St. Paul and reenact his words, continued. "Now what you worship as something unknown I am going to proclaim to you. The God who made the world and everything in it is the Lord of heaven and earth and does not live in temples built by hands." He motioned with his arm to the temples of stone which sat behind him on the high Acropolis and then down to the Hephaisteion, a monumental work of human art that had survived nearly twenty-four centuries, which sat below him. "And he is not served by human hands, as if he needed anything, because he himself gives all men life and breath and everything else. From one man he made every nation of men, that they should inhabit the whole earth; and he determined the times set for them and the exact places where they should live."

Kristen's nerves tingled. "The path of life. . ." she whispered and Paul squeezed her closer to him, understanding and agreeing with her unspoken thought. They had walked more than just the little stone and concrete path of Theorias Way to reach this spot; they had walked a path from San Francisco to reach this windy hilltop and it was exactly where they were meant to be.

"God did this so that men would seek him," the man lifted his arms in seeking, "and perhaps reach out for him," the St. Paul reached with his hands, "and find him," he closed his hands and brought them lovingly, as if he possessed the most precious thing in the world, close to his heart, "though he is not far from each one of us."

His eyes, his hurting, caring, loving eyes smiled at them, implored them, reached out to all the people of the world who were gathered on that hilltop, and Kristen and Paul knew as the St. Paul continued to the say the words of the real St. Paul that a force much greater than the wind was blowing around them. Something invisible, but Something tangible was binding them all together and instructing them and loving them; and Kristen looked at Paul and Paul looked at Kristen and they both knew that their quest for that Unknown, Something More had been realized on this windy hilltop.

And they knew that it was 'the God who made the world and everything in it' for whom they had traveled so far together to find. They had quested after Him and they had found Him on this beautiful Hill of Ares above the modern and ancient city of Athens.

And, as the St. Paul concluded the speech of that great apostle to the Gentiles by gently bowing his head, Kristen and Paul knew that their lives would never be the same again.

With hands that shook slightly, Paul turned to the seventeenth chapter and read what was written after St. Paul's speech ended.

". . .At that, Paul left the Council. A few men became followers of Paul and believed. Among them was Dionysius, a member of the Areopagus, also a woman named Damaris, and a number of others." His words ended with wonder in his tone.

Slowly, Paul looked up from the written Word and turning to Kristen, looked deeply into her eyes and said, "Kristen, like Dionysius of before. . .I believe."

"Oh, Paul. . .like Damaris of before. . .I believe too!"

With their hands clasped together they sat with faces that reflected their euphoria over discovering and recognizing the Unknown God—the God who made the world and everything in it.

People had started to talk and to move around on the hill again, but it was some moments before Paul and Kristen realized that the man who had reenacted the speech of St. Paul's so convincingly had moved next to them and was standing above them. The hem of his robe billowed out in the wind and brushed against Kristen's ankle.

Together, they turned to him and smiled. He returned their smile and said, "I feel that it is for you two that I was led to this windy hilltop today."

"Who. . ." Kristen began and then pausing, licked her lips, "who led you?"

"The same One who led you here," he replied simply.

Paul stood and pulled Kristen up with him. He towered over the smaller man but the smaller man seemed every bit as big.

"We have been searching for Something More in life, something that was unknown to us. We now understand that that Something More is definitely God."

"Alleluia!" The man shouted out, surprising both of them but rather than feeling embarrassed or ashamed by the outburst, both Kristen and Paul would have liked to have shouted out the same with him. Instead, they both grinned widely.

"But where do we go from here?" Paul asked.

"We have a Bible," Kristen offered.

"Several Bibles." Paul laughed and explained, "Until two weeks ago we didn't even own one."

"The Bible is the place to learn all about God. It is His word to us," he paused. "But first. . .how about if we pray?"

The man took both of their hands and there on the hilltop

both Kristen and Paul asked the Lord Jesus to come into their lives and to live with them forever.

"Don't ever forget," the St. Paul reminded them after their prayer, "that Jesus came to seek and to save what was lost."

"I was truly lost," Kristen said, "and it wasn't a very nice feeling."

"But a feeling neither you nor I will ever have again," Paul said and squeezed her hand.

"Amen to that!" the St. Paul exclaimed and motioned over at a group of people that were obviously waiting to talk to him. "Forgive me. . .but I must move on. Maybe," he squeezed their shoulders fondly like a brother might do, "there will be another Dionysius and Damaris to be found."

Paul and Kristen shook hands with him. "Thank you. Thank you very much."

The St. Paul started to turn away but then he looked back at them and with a twinkle in his deep, deep eyes said, "You know, a good relationship with God is the cement that holds marriages together," and before either of them could comment, he turned away from them.

Kristen's mouth hung open in shock but not Paul's. Slowly, he turned to her and with infinite love radiating from deep within his being, he drew her close to his heart and gently cradled her within her arms. The wind whispered around them, caressed them, and seemed to push them together. But even more than the physical wind was that invisible thread, that spiritual force which they now knew was God, who drew them tightly together and bound them one to another.

And knowing that it was now right to do so, knowing from the deep groanings of his soul that had been answered by the St. Paul's words, Paul reached into his pocket and pulled out a small box that was delicately wrapped in silver paper with two white rosebuds made of the finest silk intertwined atop it. He handed the box to Kristen. "He's right, Kristen. A good relationship with God is the cement that binds marriages together. I've always known that our quest was important not only to our own personal lives but for whatever life we might share. . .together."

"Oh, Paul. . ." She held the box and looked from it to Paul. She knew what it contained. And she knew what he was about to ask. And with her heart beating freely and more happily than she had ever thought it possibly could, she also knew what her answer would be.

"Kristen. . ." he paused and his eyes smiled, his mouth smiled, his whole being smiled at her. Her soul responded with a smile that brightly encouraged him to continue. "Would you do me the honor of becoming my wife?"

She threw her arms around his neck and together with the wind, whispered into his ear, "Yes, Paul. . .oh yes!"

He squeezed her to him. He felt as though his feet had left the earth and he was soaring through the evening glow with the swallows. The wind pushed them together and he knew that nothing could ever pull them apart. He loved Kristen with a love that he had never thought possible and he knew that it was because it was a love that had the backing of the One who was love. "Darling Kristen. . .so the ring of love includes us after all."

Kristen stepped back from him to look into his eyes. "I think I knew that it would from the moment you told me the story. We just had to learn about God and accept his Son as our Lord before we could let our love become a part of the history of the ring of love. It would have been," she paused and searched around for the right words, "kind of. . .backwards otherwise. After all, Christina and Paul loved God first and it was to God that Christina looked for the safety of her beloved."

"And it was because of her love and faith that he did return to her," he motioned to the package that still remained unopened in her slender hands, "and brought her this ring. Please open it."

Excitement bubbled up in her. The people on the hill faded into the background so that only she and Paul and the God who was no longer unknown to them remained. Slowly, knowing that this was one of the golden moments in life, she untied the ribbon, careful not to disturb the intertwined roses which she would keep forever, safe for her great-great-grand-daughter, and slid her finger beneath the silver paper. But before she opened the lid of the blue jeweler's box, she looked up at Paul and said, "I love you, Paul. . .I always will."

He pursed his lips together in emotion and reaching out, he gently cradled her chin in his hand. "And I promise. . .never to let anything or anyone ever come between us. Not ever." She nodded, sure that he would always remain true to his promise, and looking back down at the box which contained the symbol of their love, the symbol of past loves too, she gently pushed back the lid and rested her eyes upon the ring of love.

She gasped slightly but remained speechless. The circular emerald that glinted from the velvet box was warm and restful like a lazy spring day and yet as mysterious and timeless as the earth from which it was taken. It wasn't fiery but it was warm, and it wasn't icy but it was cool, speaking of all that must make up the love between a man and a woman. A tem-perance, a gentle sharing, a gentle love of giving and accept-ing one to the other. The emerald, flanked by diamonds and set among the strength of platinum, was an exquisite piece of jewelry.

"It's beautiful. . ." Kristen finally whispered and removing it from the box, handed it to Paul. He looked at her in ques-tion.

"As my great-great-grandfather Paul did for his Christina, would you please put this ring on my finger?"

Paul took the ring and as it caught the setting rays of the giant sun as it set in the Grecian sky, Paul pushed the family heirloom onto the ring finger of Kristen's left hand. He looked from it to her eyes and knew that he hadn't been wrong in comparing her eyes to the emerald's beauty. But he also knew that the stone was a pale reflection in comparison. She had life in her eyes, something the stone could never hope to have. And with a longing that caught Paul almost unaware, he knew that he wanted to marry Kristen as soon as possible.

"Marry me, Kristen. This week."

With her left hand gleaming its joy in its new adornment she reached up and ran her fingertips across his cheek. "Yes, Paul. Whenever you want." She agreed simply and in so doing, knew that she was following the path of her life that had been laid down for her since the beginning of time. And as Paul wrapped her in his arms and they lowered themselves to sit and watch the sun as it slipped into its bed for the night, both reluctant to leave the wondrous site of their discovery of both God and one another, Kristen knew that she was doing exactly the right thing. For a fleeting moment, she wondered how her aunt would react to their news, but it was only fleeting, because to her, all that mattered at the moment was Paul and the God who had brought them together.

And she knew that if she could have, she would have married Paul that night.

fifteen

"Oh, Melissa. . .Luke. . .he's perfect!" Kristen said to the proud parents about the little bundle of baby boy she held in her arms the next morning. Walking over to Paul, she held the baby up for him to see and he automatically cooed a few baby phrases along with her.

Looking with love at his wife, Luke commented, "We traveled a very long road to become the family we are today. I really fought Melissa. . .and God." A sadness crossed over his face. "I fought him and I blamed him for things that I shouldn't have."

"How did you finally come to understand who He was?" Paul asked.

Luke laughed. "I finally realized that I had read every medical book I could get my hands on, tomes and tomes of books, hundreds of thousands of words, and yet, I had never read the book," he looked over at Melissa, "that my dear lady here had been begging me to read." He turned back to Paul. "I finally read the Bible and I believed it. But," he laughed, "I don't know how Melissa had the patience to wait so long for me."

With love in her expressive amber eyes for the father of her child, Melissa softly replied, "Oh, I think you know very well where my patience came from."

Luke nodded and Melissa smiled at her husband before turning to Paul and Kristen. She stretched out her hand with its hospital bracelet dangling from her wrist to touch the ring on Kristen's finger. Kristen had told her all about Paul and her love and their quest before the men had arrived that morning, and Melissa was thrilled for her friend, especially since God was the foundation of their relationship.

"But you two are truly blessed to have your love happen so quickly and under such good circumstances. To have given yourselves to Christ and to become engaged all in one evening. . ." she shook her head, her long, nearly black hair shimmered like silk in the morning light, "that's a miracle, I'd say."

Kristen grimaced. "I just hope my aunt thinks it's a miracle."

Paul drew his brows together. She had mentioned to him earlier her apprehension over Aphrodite's response to their engagement.

"Kristen—she will be thrilled for us." Paul had no doubts that what he spoke was the truth.

Kristen shook her head. She wasn't convinced. "I don't know, Paul. . .she wasn't too pleased with the idea of our spending an evening together. . . How will she react to an engagement?" Kristen just couldn't get out of her head that look of soul-stopping dread that had filled the older woman's face and her doubts wouldn't be relieved until after they told Aphrodite about their engagement, something they were planning on doing immediately after church.

Paul placed his arm around her shoulder and squeezed her close to him. "Don't worry. Nothing will ever come between us." Kristen smiled up at him. She wanted to believe that more than anything in the world. But as much as she didn't want to admit it, those old doubts of her being kept from happiness assailed her. Holding the baby close to her, she wondered if she and Paul would ever be so blessed as to have a baby of their own.

"Have you set a date for your wedding?" Luke asked, cutting in on her thoughts.

Paul and Kristen looked at one another and grinned.

"Well. . ." Kristen turned to Melissa. "That depends. . .when are you getting out of the hospital?"

Melissa's eyes opened wide. Carefully she answered, "Tomorrow morning."

Kristen looked at Paul and when he nodded yes, Kristen replied. "Well. . .we had thought to get married a couple of days after you came out of the hospital. So I guess we'll be getting married on Friday."

"What?" Melissa's eyes opened wide in wonder and joyful surprise.

"I do need a matron of honor, after all." She put the little baby into her friend's arms.

"Oh, Kristen. . .I'd be honored!" She looked up at her husband and exclaimed, "What a week this has been! First our little baby is born, then Kristen's surprise visit, and now a wedding!"

Luke smiled, a special twinkle in his dark eyes for his wife.

"I'd say it's a week of miracles."

Luke and Melissa grinned at one another. They both knew that there was a time when the scientist in Luke would never have said such a thing. They both now rejoiced in his belief. It was the greatest miracle of all.

ﾞ

Looking at the pastor standing below the stained glass window that depicted the life of Christ and the spreading of His news into the world even to including a panel of St. Paul preaching to the Athenians on the Areopagus, Kristen could hardly believe that it was the same nearly drowned man whom she and Paul had pulled from the Pacific Ocean just a few short weeks ago.

With sandy blond hair and all-American good looks, Pastor Dean was a remarkably handsome man. Tall and husky, and built like an American football player, Kristen was amazed that she had had the strength to pull him onto the beach below her home. But smiling to herself, she now understood fully where her strength had come from. Her eyes moved again to the stained glass window above the pastor's head. God had been with them on that beach and He had saved not only the pastor from the waters of the earth's biggest ocean, but Paul and herself from the world's biggest lie, that made people believe that they could live a full life without God.

Kristen knew better now. And she smiled as she thought about Pastor Dean's message this morning. About the brotherhood of all believers; it had touched a sensitive chord in her heart and it was as if he had spoken right to her. That need to have blood relatives which had been all-important to her a few weeks ago was now washed away in the understanding that all believers were her relatives. She was still very glad to have her aunt, a blood relative by human consent, but she now understood that she had a multitude of other relatives in the Lord to whom the blood of Christ bound her, brothers and sisters in the Lord.

She glanced up at Paul and then down at the ring that glittered on her finger. Paul, her Paul, the man sitting at her side had put it on her finger not twenty-four hours before. It was a symbol of their love and a symbol of the love of others of her blood who had loved before them. She rubbed her finger over the hard smoothness of the circular emerald. The ring of love. Their quest had made them a part of that circular ring of love.

Seeing the direction of her gaze, Paul reached over and placed his hand over hers and together they rubbed the historic stone. She looked up at him and they smiled at one another. Kristen never before realized that people were allowed to be so happy.

Around them, people stood for the benediction. Paul and Kristen stood with them and bowing their heads prayed. Music played as the service ended and Pastor Dean smiled at them as he passed them on his way down the aisle. A soft murmur started as the congregation greeted one another with smiles and good cheer and slowly moved down the aisle to the exit of the church.

Kristen and Paul stood off to the side and waited for the congregation to greet Pastor Dean before greeting him themselves. He finished greeting the last person and with a beaming face, reached out his hands and enfolded Kristen in a hug such as a brother might give his much-loved sister.

"Kristen, Paul told me all your news on the phone this morning. Welcome, my dear sister in Christ."

Kristen pressed her check to his. "Thank you, Pastor Dean."

Pastor Dean laughed, an infectious laugh, "No, it's me that's happy to finally be able to thank you in person for pulling me out of the Pacific Ocean. How can I ever repay you?"

Kristen tilted her head to the side and, casting an impish

look at Paul before turning back to the pastor said, "Well. . . how about officiating at Paul's and my marriage next Friday?"

Dean smiled. "To officiate at your wedding would be my honor, Kristen—" He turned to Paul and took his arm above the elbow in a heartfelt shake. "My honor indeed, Paul."

❧

It was hot, hot and windy, by the time Kristen and Paul turned into the driveway of Aphrodite's neoclassical mansion. The cicadas were grinding their feet and making a racket of sound in the pine trees around the house that was nearly deafening. For the first time since coming to Greece, Kristen felt the heat, and thought with longing about San Francisco's notoriously cool summers. She remembered how Mark Twain had written that the coldest winter he ever spent was one summer in San Francisco. She smiled at how apt a description that was as she dragged her heat-drained body up the marble steps that seemed to have heat radiating up from them, like bricks in an oven. Not even the strong Meltemia could ease the furnace-like heat of the day. It felt as though someone was fanning flames over the city.

But Kristen was honest with herself and knew that more than the heat, it was the dread she felt over telling Aphrodite about Paul's and her engagement that made her feel tired and lethargic and if the truth were to be known, downright scared. Some instinct seemed to be trying to warn Kristen that the older woman was not going to take the news with joy. She paused on her climb up the stairs and lifted her hair off of her shoulders. The wind brushed against the damp curls and cooled her slightly.

"Is the heat getting to you?" Paul asked as he came up next to her.

Kristen shook her head. "It is hot today but. . .mostly, I'm apprehensive about telling Thea about us—"

"Kristen—" he smiled at her crookedly and reaching out for her hand, helped her to the top of the stairs before turning her to face him. "There will be no problems. Aphrodite will be thrilled to learn that we are to marry."

But doubt remained in Kristen's eyes. "I don't know, Paul. . ."

"Didn't I tell you that no one would ever stand between us?"

Kristen hesitantly nodded.

"Well—that includes my godmother, your aunt. If she does try to cause a problem—something I feel certain she won't do—we will still remain together and we will be married next Friday."

Kristen bit her lower lip in apprehension and as he guided her into the coolness of the marble hall, she leaned her head wearily against his shoulder. "I hope you're right."

He tapped the tip of her nose and smiled. "I'm sure that I am."

He directed her in the direction of the living room. "Now go sit down and cool off. I'll go find something cool for us to drink and be back in a minute. When Aphrodite wakes up from her afternoon siesta," his eyes seemed to dance his delight over the news they had to impart, and Kristen was sure that as much as she was dreading telling Aphrodite about their engagement, Paul was looking forward to it, "we'll invite her to our wedding."

Kristen took hope from his words and as she wandered into the living room she began to feel as though she was being ridiculous.

Her aunt had no reason not to be thrilled over their news. What could be more to the older woman's liking than to see her much-loved godson marry her long-lost niece? Aunt Aphrodite had been the personification of kindness since Kristen had come to visit, and Kristen felt as though her search for a blood relative had been fully realized in the person of her aunt. That the older woman loved her was obvious.

Kristen wandered over to the little painting by El Greco and she thought about the history that had taken place in the very room in which she now stood. Her father had grown up here, he had celebrated holidays and birthdays and graduations in this room. He had tried to celebrate his wedding in this room, but that celebration had led to his leaving the room, the house, and the country, never to return.

Kristen sighed.

Maybe, Kristen thought, *by telling of my and Paul's desire to marry, all that had been made so wrong all those years ago could finally be made right.*

She held up her left hand and ran the fingers of her right hand over and around the perfect workmanship of the round emerald that flashed in the afternoon light with all the brilliance of the God-made earth in its color.

The ring of love. . .

Perhaps the ring of love had finally come full circle and the daughter of the woman that had been spurned was to weld it back together.

Kristen held the ring higher. The sun caught its angles and flashed.

Too late, Kristen realized that it was flashing a warning. With a voice barely able to contain rage, her aunt walked up to her side and exclaimed, "What are you doing with that ring?"

sixteen

Kristen whirled to face the older woman. Even more than the anger that was detectable in the older woman's voice was the soul-stopping dread that was now openly visible in her flashing eyes.

"Thea. . . ?"

"I asked you a question." Her voice was like steel, and for the first time, Kristen understood precisely what went into making her aunt the formidable businesswoman she had become. "What are you doing with that ring?"

Kristen looked down at the ring. The platinum now seemed to burn into her flesh. She berated herself for not listening to her instinct. She had known, had sensed somehow, that Aphrodite didn't want Paul and her becoming more involved than just as friends. The question was, *Why?* It was that answer that now began to terrify Kristen. Why was Aphrodite so afraid of them becoming close? She looked back at the older woman. All traces of love and friendship and family ties seemed to have been wiped clean from the older woman's face. Kristen could only think that her grandfather must have looked the same when he sent her parents away.

That thought sent chills down Kristen's spine.

"Did Paul give you that ring?" The older woman ground out between lips that were white with anger.

"I did." Both women heard Paul answer from behind them, and Kristen couldn't have hidden the sigh of relief that emanated from her if she had tried. She was grateful when he placed the drinks he was carrying on the coffee table and came to stand by her side.

Aphrodite's eyes flashed in pain, in anger, but mostly in dread, up to Paul's. She reached for Kristen's hand and pulled it roughly with a strength Kristen didn't know the older woman possessed, up for them all to behold the offending ring. "What does this mean?" She ground out.

Paul gently removed Kristen's hand from Aphrodite's grasp and held it lovingly in his own. "It means exactly what you think it means, Nona." He spoke softly and in marked contrast to the savagery in Aphrodite's face, in her voice. "Kristen and I are to be married."

"Married!" The older woman spat out. "How dare you get involved with my niece!"

Paul's eyes narrowed. He was confused. And getting angry. "What. . . ?"

"I trusted you with my niece." She shot out.

Paul smiled and the anger he was beginning to feel vanished as suddenly as it had appeared. He thought that he now understood what she was concerned with and he was glad that he was honestly able to relieve her fears. "Then you have nothing to fear. I know it's an old-fashioned term but—" Paul looked over at Kristen and smiled. "I respect your niece. Nothing has happened between us that should only happen after marriage."

"Thank God. . ." the older woman breathed out and walking heavily over to her favorite chair, sank into its protective comfort.

Paul put his arm around Kristen and smiled reassuringly down at her as if to say, "There. The problem is solved." But Kristen didn't feel reassured. Kristen only felt as though history was about to repeat itself and for some deep reason that only the past and Aphrodite knew, she was going to be kept from happiness with Paul.

Paul explained to Aphrodite. "Kristen and I fell in love while we were in California."

"So suddenly."

Paul grimaced and calmly responded, "Sudden love has been known to happen in your family before, Nona." He indicated the ring on Kristen's finger. "Remember—Paul and Christina."

Aphrodite nodded and seemed to be looking into another time.

"Yes. . .Paul and Christina. . .and. . .others. . ." Then she looked at Paul and the anguish in her eyes was real and strong and sliced through Kristen's heart. Her words made the cut even deeper. "But why didn't you say anything to me about your," she looked from Kristen to Paul, "your. . .relationship? I might have been able to prevent so much unhappiness."

"What do you mean?" The steel in Paul's voice was ominous. He didn't like the direction the conversation was taking again.

Aphrodite looked at Paul with that determined quality, that formidable quality that brooked no argument, that steel-like quality which was a match for his own. He saw it and recognized it for what it was.

Kristen saw it and quaked. She knew that somehow, something that that woman was going to say was going to keep her from a future with Paul. She could feel it in her very being.

Finally the older woman spoke, but that instinct Kristen should have listened to before was now warning her that her aunt was prevaricating and trying to hide the truth. "You are my godson. In the eyes of the church that is the same as being my son. That makes you. . ." she seemed to stumble over the word and swallowed, "cousins. A marriage between the two of you will never be permitted."

Paul laughed. "That's archaic."

Aphrodite's eyebrows cut a straight line across her face. Paul's cut a straight line across his in answer.

"Nevertheless. . .marriage between you two will not be allowed." She spoke as if she was the empress of the land, decreeing their lives.

"Aphrodite. . ." Paul began slowly. If she was the empress, he was the emperor. Tone for tone, steel for steel, soul for soul, Paul matched Aphrodite, and Kristen thought that it was as though they were the same person.

And it was then that Kristen understood.

It was then that she finally understood the truth.

And the knowledge of it sliced through her heart with all the pain of a dull blade and even as she heard Paul tell the older woman in no uncertain terms that they were going to be married the following Friday, Kristen knew that it was the older woman who spoke the truth.

She and Paul would never be allowed to marry.

Not in any church.

Stepping back from Paul, Kristen raised her hand to her mouth and bit deeply into her finger to try and keep from crying out. But she couldn't have muffled the cry that came out of her with anything. A strangled cry, it was a cry that came from her soul, a cry of anguish for a love that could never be.

"*No!*"

Paul was by her side. "Kristen.. darling. . .don't. . .it will be all right." He looked over at Aphrodite, imploring her to stop hurting Kristen and as Aphrodite looked back at him, obviously wanting with all her might to stop her hurting words, Kristen wondered, through the cloud of pain that enveloped her, how she hadn't seen the resemblance between the two of them immediately.

It wasn't anything physical because by some trick of genetics Paul didn't resemble Aphrodite in the least. Rather, it went deeper than looks, it was as if their souls were the same, the parts that think and act and reason were identical.

Aphrodite looked away from Paul and met Kristen's eyes. In them now there was no empress. Just an old woman that was sorry, very, very sorry for the hurt history had to inflict on the two people she loved most in the world. Kristen saw it and reached out her hand to her. She somehow knew that the older woman, the woman who had never relied on anyone's strength but her own, needed her strength now, the strength Kristen had to give only because of her new faith in God.

"Oh, Thea. . ." Kristen whispered and gently squeezed the frail hand of her aunt, "I don't know why I didn't see it immediately." Tears formed in Aphrodite's crinkled eyes as she realized that Kristen had guessed her secret. "I'm so sorry Christina. . .so sorry. . ." she croaked out in a voice that was little more than a whisper.

Kristen nodded and motioned to Paul. "You must tell him. . ." she whispered.

"Tell me what?" Paul ground out and turned to his god-mother. He was angry now, angry and confused.

Aphrodite suddenly looked old. Like an old warrior who had fought her last battle. In truth, she had battled throughout life so that this moment would never have to be faced. She glanced down at the ring on her niece's hand, the ring of love. It had turned and twisted to bring them to this moment, this moment that Aphrodite had hoped never to arrive at.

"Tell him." Kristen gently prodded and squeezed her aunt's hand to give her the strength to speak the words that would forever keep Kristen from the man she loved.

"Tell me what?" Paul ground out again.

Aphrodite turned her tired old eyes to Paul. "That I'm your biological mother."

 za

Kristen pushed the door of her home closed against the cold and wet November wind that blew off the Pacific Ocean. Crossing over to her living room, she placed her briefcase down next to the coffee table, intending on going over some papers during the long Thanksgiving Day weekend. Her glance rested on her little statue of the *Youth of Antikythera* before sliding away to the well-worn Bible that rested beneath it. Because of the Bible, Kristen was able to smile at the little statue.

When she'd first returned to California after learning that Paul was her first cousin, Kristen had hidden the statue away in her closet, the memories it invoked too painful for her to face. But gradually, because of the Bible, she was able to bring the little statue out and look at it and remember Paul, her aunt's son, with joy.

She no longer talked to the little statue as she once did. Rather, because of the quest she and Paul had taken together, their search for that Unknown, Something More, she now talked regularly to the God who was no longer unknown to her. Kristen knew that without that wonderful life-saving, personal relationship with God that was growing deeper and more precious with each passing day she would never have been able to survive leaving Paul. That she was related by blood to Paul was one of the great ironies of life. She had been desperate for blood relatives, had yearned for them. But finding out that Paul and she were too closely related to marry brought a sadness unlike anything she had ever known before. And she still couldn't quite believe it. Her feelings for him had never been cousinly.

Kristen kicked off her shoes and sat heavily down on the sofa, her wool suit bending with her, and reaching forward, she picked up her Bible. Holding it as one would hold the most precious, most redeeming, most comforting thing in the world, which it had become to her, she let herself remember that last day in Athens.

After her aunt had told Paul that she was his biological mother, she had gone on to explain how she had fallen suddenly and very deeply in love with Paul's father, whose name had been David. As might be expected, Aphrodite's father was against her marrying David from the start, even though David's family was one to be admired and one which had a long-standing political friendship with the country of Greece. But despite all their pleas and all David's promises to cherish and adore and keep Aphrodite safe and happy, Aphrodite's father had adamantly refused her permission to marry the handsome Englishman.

"War raged around us." Aphrodite's tired old voice had trembled as she told about her love for Paul's natural father. "It was a time when young, healthy people were alive one day," pain gripped her face at the remembrance, "and dead the next. So many friends. . .dead. . ." her voice trailed off, remembering that sad time of war.

"Tell me—" Paul swallowed a lump which had formed in his throat as he tried to assimilate that this remarkable woman was his blood mother. A part of him admitted that he had always known that Aphrodite was his mother and her pronouncement really didn't surprise him. What was confusing him now, however, was that that same part was now crying out that Kristen was not his first cousin. Something didn't seem right about that and even though his heart was breaking thinking that there was nothing he could do to change the flow of mutual blood that filled their veins, he somehow felt that he had to learn all he could about the past, about his biological father, about Aphrodite and her family, in order to search for that missing something.

Paul Andrakos would not, could not, accept that Kristen and he had no future together. He would not accept it until he had searched and learned all that there was to know about that time and the people of that time.

Aphrodite looked at Paul and she reached out and rubbed her hand across his face as only a mother is allowed to rub her grown son. She smiled and Kristen felt that she said the words that she had longed to say for all the years of Paul's life.

"You are the image of your father," she laughed lightly. "I used to tell him that he resembled the statue of the *Youth of Antikythera* too." Her eyes sparkled as she looked back at Paul. "And he hated it too."

Paul smiled at that. Even though many men would feel anger and hurt and confusion over being told that their lineage was not what they had thought it to be, Paul loved and respected his nona, his biological mother, so much that he felt certain that she had done the best she could with the situation she had found herself in all those years ago, and so he was able to sit and wait for her to tell her story and the story of her love for the man who had fathered him.

Her face turned grave with sadness. "My father would not give David and me permission to marry," she looked at Paul with a degree of that formidable spirit which was so familiar to him, "but I loved David and he loved me so we did marry. We exchanged our wedding vows in a little medieval church overlooking the Aegean Sea. An American serviceman, who was a clergyman, officiated at our wedding but," she looked deeply into Paul's eyes, "the marriage was not one which the state of Greece, at that time, would recognize."

That news didn't bother Paul. He was sure that the marriage was legal in the sight of God and according to the American clergyman. "What happened to—my father?" he asked. That was important to him.

Sadness washed over Aphrodite's face, making her look old and frail and very, very tired. "We had one wonderful week together and then. . .he became a casualty of that dreadful, dreadful war."

Paul squeezed her hand and she looked up at him with brightness shining in her eyes. "But David left me with a gift. . .the most wonderful and beautiful gift he could have given me. He gave you to me, my son."

Tears swam in Paul's eyes as he pulled his mother into his arms and held her, as she held him, for the first time ever, as mother and son.

She pulled back after a moment to continue the story. Having begun it, she had to finish it now, all of it. It was a secret she had held for too many years and it weighed heavily upon her.

"I told my father about my marriage and about you and he was," she glanced up at Kristen, "well, let me say, he was even angrier with me than he was when Nick brought your mother to us years later, Christina."

"Oh, Thea. . ." In spite of her pain, Kristen felt for the older woman.

"But. . .how did my adoptive parents come to be my parents?" Paul needed to know. "You were all so close, such good friends."

Aphrodite nodded. "Our being good friends was a miracle. Your parents had been married for many years, and were still without the child they longed for. My father was an associate of your father's and knew of their desire. When he learned that I was pregnant he arranged it so that both your mother and I would go to live in a village. Supposedly, I went to care for your mother who, everyone was told, was finally expecting a baby. Of course, it was the other way around. But when we returned to Athens everyone thought she was the mother and I was the godmother of her beautiful baby boy. I loved your adoptive parents dearly, Paul. They were not only wonderful to you, my dear son, but wonderful to me. They knew the entire story and insisted that I be a part of your life," she grimaced, "much to my father's chagrin."

"I can imagine."

"The only time that my relationship with your parents," she paused and spoke with determination, "for they were your parents, Paul—in every way but blood—was in danger of faltering was when," Aphrodite looked up at Kristen and smiled sadly, "your father returned to Greece with his bride. I was appalled by my father's behavior and told him so. He warned me that if I became involved and sided with Nick and Jane in any way that he would tell Paul, who was just a young boy, about his parentage. So when my father demanded of your father that he give up his Jane and his unborn child, I was unable to come to his aid. Too many lives would have been hurt if Paul had been told about his lineage then."

"But. . .why didn't you tell my father the truth?" Kristen wailed. "So much pain would have been avoided."

Aphrodite shrugged her shoulders. "Looking back, it seems that that would have solved many problems but at the time," she shook her head, "I don't know. . .my father was formidable and had a mean streak in him that he never hesitated to use when crossed. All I knew was that I couldn't chance my father telling Paul. I just couldn't let that happen."

Tears fell down the lines of Aphrodite's face, following a course Kristen was sure they had followed many times before. "I just couldn't hurt," she reached out her hand and caressed Paul's face, "your dear. . .mother that way. . .nor your father. . .nor you." She looked over at Kristen. "So I remained silent when Nick looked to me for help. I remained silent," she repeated and looked across the room, across space and time to that moment, before looking back at Kristen. "And I'll never forget your father's look. To say I hurt him. . . it's not enough. I think that. . .I must have killed something within him with my silence."

"But you told him everything when you made up," Kristen reminded her, her own eyes wet with tears.

"Oh yes. . .I told him everything." She looked up at Paul. "Even that he had a grown nephew."

&

"A grown nephew. . . A grown nephew. . ." the Pacific wind seemed to shout it out as it pushed pellets of rain up against Kristen's window and made Kristen aware of the cold November day once again.

She got up and crossed over to her patio door. The Pacific Ocean was a swirling mass of water and foam, gray and foreboding, dark and cold. Kristen shivered slightly. It was exactly how she had felt that hot August afternoon when she and Paul had said good-bye.

She had accepted the news of their close blood tie almost fatalistically, as thought she had been expecting something to keep her from happiness with Paul.

But Paul hadn't.

"Kristen," he had ground out by the car that was to take her to the airport and away from him, "I don't believe that God would give us to one another only to have our relationship end so tragically."

"Paul. . ." She shook her head and tried to keep the tears from falling. But it was useless, as useless as their planning a life together had been. "Paul. . .it's hopeless. . .we. . .are cousins. First cousins. We just have to accept it."

"I do not accept it," he ground out. "I will not accept it," he repeated softer, "until I've searched all angles and found out everything that there is to know about that time. Something just isn't right. Something just doesn't fit."

Kristen looked down at her hands. "It's us that doesn't fit together," she said, and through eyes swimming with tears that blurred the emerald on her finger and made it seem bigger and more defused, Kristen tugged on the ring to remove it from her heat-swollen finger.

Paul looked at her aghast. "What are you doing?"

"Returning your ring."

"No!" He stilled her hand with his own but then quickly removed it from hers. Whenever they touched, it was as though they burned one another. "It's your ring," he reasoned. "Regardless."

She nodded. She couldn't fight him and he was right. As the only female descendant of Christina's and Paul's, the ring was hers.

But she really didn't want it. It mocked her love for Paul. "The ring of love. . ." she whispered. "I guess it doesn't include us, Paul," she said and stepped into the airport limousine.

Paul leaned his forehead against the window. "But it will, Kristen. It will. Something is wrong. Something. . .I will search and find out what it is. Please don't take the ring off until I'm satisfied that we have no future together."

She smiled bravely and nodded. If he didn't want her removing the ring, it was something she could do for him and she would do it. But she was quite certain that unlike their last search together, this one would not yield satisfactory answers.

Kristen shivered again. She wasn't sure whether it was from the cold November day or from her thoughts, but she walked over to the thermostat control and reaching out with her left hand, turned on the heater. The emerald flashed on her hand. Paul had asked her to wear it until they saw one another again. And she would. But she still thought it was useless.

She was not only cold but tired. She went into the kitchen, opened a can of tomato soup, made a grilled cheese sandwich, and then put herself to bed.

She fell asleep on that Thanksgiving Eve with a simple prayer on her lips. "Please, God. . .make everything right . . .please. . ."

seventeen

If possible, the day Kristen awoke to was even grayer and even wetter and even colder than the one which she had fallen asleep to. She looked at the clock and was shocked at the time. It was past ten o'clock!

Her eyes traveled over the photos that were in silver frames on the table. In the one Melissa held her three-month-old baby boy high in the air in a happy moment of motherhood and in the other, Lottie and the new man in her life were posed romantically besides the world-famous cliffs of Santorini.

Kristen sighed and pushed back the down comforter that had kept her warm and toasty all night. The house was cold again so she quickly washed and dressed in comfortable but warm old jeans and a sweatshirt that had Williamsburg, Virginia, emblazoned across it.

She made coffee, switched on the TV to see which of the numerous Thanksgiving Day parades she could find, but she paused in front of the set when a news story captured her attention. A reporter told the sad story about a promising athlete who was going to miss competing in the Olympic Games the following summer because of an automobile accident which had severely broken her ankle. What made the story extra sad was that it would make the third time in twelve years of trying that the runner, Niki Alexander, who had set a new world record the previous summer in middle distance running, was going to miss out on the Olympics because of injury or illness. Kristen sighed. She could feel for the girl. Such a disappointment. A disappointment which was similar to her own simply because. . .it was a deep and cutting disappointment.

Flipping the channel, wanting the happy sounds of a parade to fill the house, Kristen walked into the kitchen and got busy with making the four pumpkin pies she had promised to make for the church-sponsored Thanksgiving dinner she was going to attend later in the day.

She had found a lovely church home after returning from Greece, one which was similar to the one in Athens in that it was filled with people who loved the Lord and loved one another like one always believed blood relatives should, but often didn't. They were Kristen's relatives now, relatives given to her through the blood of the Lord rather than through the blood of ancestors and in them Kristen knew that she had finally found the relatives for whom she had been craving.

She loved her Aunt Aphrodite dearly, but she knew that it would be unwise for her to ever return to Greece. She loved her aunt's son too much for that. And not as one should love a cousin. She mixed the shortening, flour, and the salt together for her homemade pie crust and was vigorously slicing through it, her emerald ring flashing like green lightning as she worked, when she thought she heard the doorbell chime.

She paused and tilted her head to the side and waited. She wasn't expecting anyone and thought perhaps it was the TV playing tricks on her. But when it sounded again, she quickly wiped her hands on her apron, removed it, and rushed through the living room and over to the door.

She glanced through the peephole.

And *zap!*

She jumped back as though a laser had struck her!

Paul, the Paul who should have been her Paul, stood on the other side of her door.

She looked down at the ring on her finger and was amazed that at a time like this she should notice the bits of flour that were stuck to it. She was sure that Paul had come to tell her that his search had proven that it was time for her to remove the ring and she just didn't know how she could bear the pain.

She squeezed her eyes shut on the pain that threatened to overwhelm her and prayed, "Dear God, help me. . .help Paul," as she slid the security bolt free of the lock and swung open the door to the man she loved.

"Darling Kristen," he reached out his hands and took hers in his and spoke the words she had longed to hear but had thought she never would. "We are not related to one another in any way."

"What?" she breathed out the question. It was as if the days, the weeks, the months had never parted them. They were continuing their parting conversation as if it had occurred only moments before. "We aren't blood relatives?"

His dark eyes swam with moisture as he pulled her gently to him and whispered into her ear. "The only blood we share is the blood of Christ which binds all believers together in a Christian family of brotherhood."

"Oh, Paul!" The relief she felt trickled out of her eyes as all the tears of sadness gave way to tears of joy as she nuzzled her nose against the warmth of his neck, savoring the scent of him, the feel of him, and knowing that there would be a future for them after all.

"But how? You aren't Aphrodite's son after all?" And she held him closer, wondering what traumatic discoveries he had made during the last few months.

He took a deep breath and gently tilted her head to look at him. "I am Aphrodite's son."

She frowned in puzzlement. "But if you're Aphrodite's son . . .and we aren't first cousins. . ." The possibilities were staggering and she let them dangle in the wind as she hesitantly considered them.

She didn't hear the older man step up behind her until he spoke. "Hello, Kristy."

"Uncle George?!" Kristen whirred around, totally shocked to see her uncle standing behind her. "What. . . ?"

Uncle George smiled and with a twinkle in his eyes asked of Paul. "Do you want to give her these now?" From behind his back he brought out a beautiful bouquet of red roses.

"Oh, they're beautiful!" Kristen accepted them and cradled them gently in her arms before looking at the two men in total confusion. "What's going on here?"

"Let's go in the house and we'll tell you," Paul said and

putting his arm around her shoulder, he guided her into the living room.

She put her roses on the coffee table next to her Bible, took their coats, and asked of her Uncle George, "I thought you were supposed to be in China through the new year?"

"It will probably extend longer than that. I'll be returning tomorrow."

"Then why. . . ?" She looked from her uncle to Paul. "What's going on?"

Paul took her hand in his. "Remember how I told you something just didn't seem right about. . .our being cousins?"

"Yes but. . .I don't know how you even got that feeling."

"Well," Paul smiled and reached out to rub her face as only a man who loves a woman can, "other than not having cousinly feelings for you, something seemed wrong, like there was something important missing from the puzzle of our past which our ancestors had put together."

"Like what?"

"Like. . .how could a man reject and disown not only one, but two grandchildren, especially when that was all he had?"

"What do you mean?"

"I mean. . .my grandfather didn't want me because his daughter, Aphrodite, had married without his permission and had married a foreigner at that. And in the intervening years, she had made it very plain that she wouldn't ever marry again nor have other children. Then, one day his son arrives, married to a foreign woman who is expecting their first child. It just didn't make sense to me that our grandfather would make the same mistake a second time. . .unless. . .there was something more, another much bigger reason for him in his narrow-minded, bigoted way not to accept that second grandchild."

Kristen's eyes opened wide at the implications. Since Paul was Aphrodite's biological son the only way for them not to be cousins would be if Aphrodite and her father weren't siblings or she wasn't her father's biological child. The thought was staggering. She turned amazed eyes to her Uncle George, understanding now why her uncle was here.

"Uncle George? Is there something I should be aware of?"

Uncle George cleared his throat and looked uncomfortable, a trait Kristen had never seen in him before. "I wasn't sure whether I should tell you or not. I thought about it on your birthday," he reached into the breast pocket of his coat and pulled out an envelope and handed it to her, "especially when you gave me these photos, but you seemed so happy for a change and I had no idea then that Paul was your aunt's son and that there might be a problem if you two became involved so—" he paused and shrugged his shoulders much like an adolescent might when explaining why he had returned home too late, "I adopted a wait-and-see attitude."

Kristen opened the envelope and the picture on top was the one of her mother with the man with laughing green eyes and dark wavy hair who was looking at her mother as if she was the woman he loved.

And then Kristen knew.

She knew why she and Paul were not first cousins.

She knew why her uncle was there.

She looked up at George, her eyes wide and questioning. But she wasn't questioning what she had already guessed. She was questioning the how of it all.

George nodded. "Raphael was your biological father." He confirmed her knowledge. "He and your mother were to be married the week after this picture was taken. Their love was one of which fairy tales are made. They loved one another dearly and you were the product of that love, conceived, your mother told Nick and me, the day before he was killed in that Rally race. She and Nick thought of you as a gift from Raphael. . .and from God. Even more as the years wore on and they were never able to have children, most likely because of the malaria which Nick suffered when he was a teenager."

"But. . .my parents, Nick and Jane," she qualified, "loved one another dearly. I know they did."

"Yes, they did." He paused and then continued. "You see Kristy, when Raphael died in that auto crash, Jane confided in Nick that she was pregnant. It was then that Nick told her of his love for her. He had always loved her but because of his friendship with Raphael he had kept his love to himself. He begged Jane to marry him, promising to love and cherish her—and her baby—forever."

"He certainly did that." Tears swam in Kristen's eyes as she thought about the two men whom she could call father. The one had given her life, the other had sustained her life. Her mother had loved them both and so did she. It was as simple as that.

She looked down at the picture of her mother with the man who had fathered her. That her mother was in love with him was now obvious to Kristen's enlightened eyes and she was certain that she would have liked the fun-loving daredevil whose looks and blood she had inherited.

She turned to the next picture that showed the four friends all together and ran her fingertip lightly over the old photo, with a special pause for the father who had cherished and adored her and given up his family because of his love for her and her mother.

"I think I have been blessed in my fathers, in my mother, and," she looked up at the white-headed man who still looked so much like the laughing youth in the photo and putting her arms around him squeezed him as she had always done and whispered, "in my uncle."

"Dear Kristy—" he patted her back, "both your fathers would be proud of you."

She looked back at the photo of her mother and Raphael. "I look like my—father—don't I?"

George nodded. "You're the image of him. Your eyes, particularly."

"I always wondered where I got my green eyes from." But now her green eyes looked at George in hurt. "But why didn't my parents tell me?"

Uncle George shrugged his shoulders. "I don't know. Probably, they wanted to. But they just kept putting it off until—"

"—It was too late." She finished the sentence for him and

at his sad nod, she smiled. "But you know, Uncle George, at this point it doesn't even matter. In fact, the news that they had probably dreaded telling me has become the best news I could ever have. It doesn't change at all how I feel about my parents, except maybe to love them even more now that I understand what they had to go through in order to have a life together and," she reached out for Paul, "best of all—it means that Paul and I can marry!"

"And that will be accomplished within the week," Paul was quick to reassure her. "Your Aunt Aphrodite and James are planning a fabulous wedding reception."

"But not the wedding?"

"No. That she's leaving to us. She wants it to be our moment, our service, and held in whichever church or spot on this wonderful earth that we desire."

Kristen smiled but then a cloud passed over her face. "But she's not really my aunt."

Paul didn't say a word but rather reached for his briefcase and pulled out a box. He handed it to Kristen. "This is from your aunt. She said that you forgot it."

Kristen looked at him in question. He shook his head and motioned for her to open the box. She did, and gasped when she saw the old leather of Paul and Christina's Bible.

Paul took it from her and opened it to the family registrations of births and deaths. Above her name had been added Paul's name, his date of birth, and the name of his biological and adoptive parents. And next to her name was added the name of her biological father, Raphael Tores.

"In every way but by blood," Paul explained, "you are her brother Nick's child. She loves you as such and," he glanced at his watch, "she'll be calling you later to tell you."

"Oh, Paul. . ." Kristen could hardly believe that all she had hoped for, all that she had prayed for, was coming true and in a magnificent way whereby nobody got hurt. She put her arms around his shoulders and let herself lean against him. This is where she belonged and this is where she would stay forever.

Through a fog of happiness, she heard Uncle George clear

his throat. "Well, I'm glad that I rented my own car. I'm going to leave you two lovebirds and be on my way."

Kristen turned to him. "Oh, but Uncle George. . .it's Thanksgiving. Won't you celebrate with us?"

He reached out and rubbed her cheek. "Darling Kristy, I think I just did." She smiled as the two men chuckled and shook hands.

"Thank you, sir, for all your help." Paul said.

"I still don't know how you tracked me down. I was quite literally at the end of the earth."

Kristen laughed, that light tinkling sound that made both men happy. "Believe me, Uncle George, when Paul goes on a search, he doesn't stop until he's found what he's looking for."

After her uncle left, with promises to try and attend their wedding, Paul took Kristen's hand and walked with her to look out at the churning ocean. His thumb played with the emerald ring on her finger, hers joined in with his.

Kristen spoke softly. "I've often stood here and thought about Christina and how she probably stood looking out at the churning sea below Galaxidi, turning and twisting her ring and wondering whether she would ever see her Paul again." Kristen took her eyes away from the sea and looked up at Paul, her green eyes soft and full of light. "And I wondered the same thing. . .whether I would ever see my Paul again."

"Darling Kristen," he pulled her tightly against his side. "The ring of love has turned and twisted to finally include us in its loving history—for that we have only God to thank."

Kristen nodded and rested her head against his chest. "Only God—Who showed us our paths—"

"—And made our paths run together."

A Letter To Our Readers

Dear Reader:

In order that we might better contribute to your reading enjoyment, we would appreciate your taking a few minutes to respond to the following questions. When completed, please return to the following:

Rebecca Germany, Managing Editor
Heartsong Presents
P.O. Box 719
Uhrichsville, Ohio 44683

1. Did you enjoy reading *Odyssey of Love?*
   ❏ Very much. I would like to see more books
   by this author!
   ❏ Moderately
   I would have enjoyed it more if _____

   _____

2. Are you a member of **Heartsong Presents**? ❏Yes ❏No
   If no, where did you purchase this book?_____

   _____

3. What influenced your decision to purchase this
   book? (Check those that apply.)

   ❏ Cover   ❏ Back cover copy

   ❏ Title   ❏ Friends

   ❏ Publicity   ❏ Other_____

4. How would you rate, on a scale from 1 (poor) to 5
   (superior), the cover design? _____

5. On a scale from 1 (poor) to 10 (superior), please rate
   the following elements.

   ___Heroine   ___Plot

   ___Hero   ___Inspirational theme

   ___Setting   ___Secondary characters

6. What settings would you like to see covered in
   Heartsong Presents books?_____

   _____

   _____

7. What are some inspirational themes you would like
   to see treated in future books?_____

   _____

   _____

8. Would you be interested in reading other **Heartsong
   Presents** titles?   ❏ Yes   ❏ No

9. Please check your age range:
   ❏ Under 18   ❏ 18-24   ❏ 25-34
   ❏ 35-45   ❏ 46-55   ❏ Over 55

10. How many hours per week do you read? _____

Name _____

Occupation _____

Address_____

City_____ State_____ Zip _____

······· Presents ·······

Great Inspirational Romance at a Great Price!

Heartsong Presents books are inspirational romances in contemporary and historical settings, designed to give you an enjoyable, spirit-lifting reading experience. You can choose wonderfully written titles from some of today's best authors like Veda Boyd Jones, Yvonne Lehman, Tracie J. Peterson, Nancy N. Rue, and many others.

When ordering quantities less than twelve, above titles are $2.95 each.